SPECIAL MESSAGE TO READERS

This book is published under the auspices of

THE ULVERSCROFT FOUNDATION

(registered charity No. 264873 UK)

Established in 1972 to provide funds for research, diagnosis and treatment of eye diseases.
Examples of contributions made are: —

A Children's Assessment Unit at Moorfield's Hospital, London.

•

Twin operating theatres at the Western Ophthalmic Hospital, London.

•

A Chair of Ophthalmology at the Royal Australian College of Ophthalmologists.

•

The Ulverscroft Children's Eye Unit at the Great Ormond Street Hospital For Sick Children, London.

You can help further the work of the Foundation by making a donation or leaving a legacy. Every contribution, no matter how small, is received with gratitude. Please write for details to:

THE ULVERSCROFT FOUNDATION,
The Green, Bradgate Road, Anstey,
Leicester LE7 7FU, England.
Telephone: (0116) 236 4325

In Australia write to:

THE ULVERSCROFT FOUNDATION,
c/o The Royal Australian and New Zealand College of Ophthalmologists,
94-98 Chalmers Street, Surry Hills,
N.S.W. 2010, Australia

Melinda Hammond lives in a farmhouse on the edge of the Pennines. Her interests include theatre and music, and supporting her son's go-kart racing team.
To find out more visit the author's website at www.myweb.tiscali.co.uk/melham

A RATIONAL ROMANCE

England, 1803. Elliot Malvern, seventh Marquis of Ullenwood, is very content with his bachelor lifestyle, spending his fortune on the pleasurable pursuits of gambling and mistresses. Rosamond Beaumarsh is determined to remain unmarried and independent. What, then, could persuade them to plunge into an adventure that takes them to post-revolutionary Paris and flings them into a headlong flight across France? Only the exercise of logic. The pair embark upon a romantic adventure and learn that rational thought has very little to do with true love . . .

Books by Melinda Hammond
Published by The House of Ulverscroft:

SUMMER CHARADE
FORTUNE'S LADY
AUTUMN BRIDE
THE HIGHCLOUGH LADY
A LADY AT MIDNIGHT
DANCE FOR A DIAMOND
GENTLEMEN IN QUESTION
THE BELLES DAMES CLUB

MELINDA HAMMOND

A RATIONAL ROMANCE

Complete and Unabridged

ULVERSCROFT
Leicester

First published in Great Britain in 2007 by
Robert Hale Limited
London

First Large Print Edition
published 2008
by arrangement with
Robert Hale Limited
London

British Library CIP Data

Hammond, Melinda
A rational romance.—Large print ed.—
Ulverscroft large print series: historical romance
1. Great Britain—History—George III, *1760 – 1820*
—Fiction 2. Paris (France)—History—*1799 – 1815*
—Fiction 3. Love stories 4. Large type books
I. Title
823.9′2 [F]

ISBN 978–1–84782–363–2

Published by
F. A. Thorpe (Publishing)
Anstey, Leicestershire

Set by Words & Graphics Ltd.
Anstey, Leicestershire
Printed and bound in Great Britain by
T. J. International Ltd., Padstow, Cornwall

This book is printed on acid-free paper

1

'Damn you Ullenwood. You win again.'

Elliot Malvern, seventh Marquis of Ullenwood, smiled as he reached out and pulled the pile of rouleaux towards him.

'It's the luck of the cards, Ashby.'

'And you have had more than your share of it this past se'ennight,' grumbled Sir James Ashby. 'I wish I had stayed in the country.'

'Nonsense, James,' murmured the marquis, a gleam of amusement in his hard eyes. 'Playing spillikins or pitch and toss with your nephews? I hardly think so.'

'You are right, of course,' said Sir James gloomily. 'I am always happy to spend Christmas with m'sister, but after a week I am itching to get back to Town.'

'No doubt you told her you had work to do,' murmured the marquis.

Sir James wagged a finger at him.

'You may mock, Elliot, but there is always something to be done at the Foreign Office. And don't you be thinking that the peace with France has made matters any easier. Damned patched-up piece of nonsense — I cannot bear to think of it.'

‘Then do not,’ retorted Lord Ullenwood. ‘Concentrate on the cards instead. It might improve your game.’

‘Little chance of that when you are on such good form,’ growled Sir James. He signalled to the footman to refill his glass. ‘You have the devil’s own luck with cards and women, Elliot. The first I put down to your intellect; the latter, well, ’tis a mystery to me: you love ’em and leave ’em, and there’s still more ready to fall at your feet.’

‘The ones I — er — love and leave, as you so eloquently put it, James, do very well while they are under my protection.’

‘But none of ’em stays under your protection for long.’

‘No. As soon as they begin to bore me, I give them their *congé*.’

A gentleman in a powdered bag-wig snorted.

‘You are a cold-hearted devil, Ullenwood.’

‘Merely a rational one, Leighton. Emotion clouds the brain. I do not allow my mistresses such power over me.’ He smiled. ‘I like to keep a clear head for my gambling.’

‘Talking of gambling,’ said Sir James, ‘I suppose you will be at Northby’s tomorrow night? The talk is that the play is going to be very deep — starting at midnight.’

‘I might look in.’

‘I heard Northby is quite done-up. Bailiffs will be closing on him any day now,’ remarked Mr Leighton, the gentleman in the bag-wig.

‘So why go?’ asked Sir James.

‘My dear Ashby, everyone who likes deep play will be there!’ cried a stout baronet. ‘Brooks’s and White’s will be empty tomorrow night.’

‘Then let us hope the evening lives up to its promise,’ murmured Lord Ullenwood. He shook back the ruffles at his wrists and picked up a fresh pack of cards. ‘Another game, gentlemen?’

⋆ ⋆ ⋆

The windows of the grand house blazed with light illuminating the impressive portico, but no torches burned at the edges of the drive. Although the darkness might hide the weeds encroaching on the gravel, it could not disguise the pot-holes, and the final few yards of the journey were very uncomfortable for the occupants of the various carriages pulling up at the entrance. Lord Ullenwood entered the great hall and was shown up to the Red Saloon, a large apartment on the first floor where he was greeted at the door by Sir James Ashby, who was surveying the scene with a moody scowl.

'Evening, Elliot. What do you think Northby is about this evening? No ladies invited, no supper laid on.'

The marquis shrugged, his keen eyes surveying the scene.

'Northby is devoting the evening to play, Ashby. Food and females would merely be a distraction.'

'Damn it all, even Almack's provides supper!'

'I have no doubt you will survive, my friend.' Lord Ullenwood reached out, took a glass of wine from the tray of a passing waiter and sipped it. 'At least the wine is tolerable.'

Their host came up at that moment and the gentlemen turned to greet him.

'Lord Ullenwood . . . Sir James.' Lord Northby bowed stiffly, his upright bearing belying his advanced years.

'My lord.' Sir James waved towards the crowded room. 'Quite a crush, sir.'

Lord Northby's lip curled. 'Aye, every gambler in Town is gathered in my house tonight. They turn out quick enough if there's the chance to win a fortune.'

'Had you a special reason for this evening, my lord?' asked the marquis.

'You'll know soon enough,' muttered the old man, before moving away.

'Well!' exclaimed Sir James, watching their

host's retreating figure. 'Dashed odd behaviour — why, he has turned the house into a gambling hell for the night. Truth to tell, I have never much liked the fellow. Proud old dog, too surly for my taste. And he made some damnably cutting remarks about one of my waistcoats a few months ago. I've not forgotten.'

Lord Ullenwood's eyes drifted towards the garishly patterned creation that was displayed beneath Sir James's dark evening coat.

'Remarkable,' he murmured. 'Well, since we are here, shall we join the play?'

* * *

With so many like-minded gentlemen in the saloon, the marquis had to choose between a hand of piquet with a close acquaintance or joining a group intent on faro. From other tables came the rattle of dice boxes, but my lord decided to begin with piquet. The initial chatter in the room soon died away, replaced by quiet murmurings, with only the dealers' calls and the occasional shouts of elation or groans of despair breaking the tension. The candles were burning low in their sockets by the time the marquis made his way to the hazard table. Copious quantities of wine had had their effect on the company, many of whom were slumped in their chairs, snoring gently.

'Here comes Ullenwood,' Mr Leighton greeted him with a bleary smile. 'Will you play, my lord?'

'I believe the marquis considers hazard as his particular game.' Sir James Ashby raised his glass. 'Well, Elliot, will you join us?'

Lord Ullenwood glanced around the table. A dozen or so gentlemen were watching him, including his host. He shrugged.

'Why not?'

'I'll tell you why not,' sneered one, a gentleman with red hair and a discontented look in his pale eyes. 'Ullenwood's had the devil's own luck recently.'

'If you don't wish to play against me, Granthorpe, you can leave the table,' said the marquis.

Mr Granthorpe stood up.

'I will. I won't bet against you at hazard, Ullenwood. I've lost more than enough tonight.' With a bow he turned and walked off, swaying slightly.

'Don't mind Granthorpe,' said Sir James, 'he's drunk as a wheelbarrow. Come, I'm caster and I've called a main of six — will you set against me?'

* * *

The dice were cast and cast again: sums were wagered, won and lost until the dice box was handed to Lord Ullenwood. He threw his stake on the table, called a main of seven and threw the dice.

'*Quatre-trey*!' declared Sir James. 'Blast you, Elliot, you've nicked it. Damn your winning form!'

Lord Ullenwood continued to cast and the pile of rouleaux and notes of hand stacked on the little table beside him grew steadily. Gentlemen staked their last rouleau then left the table, groaning as the marquis continued to win.

'It seems your lordship cannot lose,' remarked his host.

Lord Ullenwood threw another stake on the table.

'The game favours those who can calculate the odds, my lord, you know that.' He picked up the dice box and rattled it gently.

'Well, man, call a main,' demanded Lord Northby, impatiently.

'Seven.'

'I'll set you,' said Lord Northby, matching the marquis's stake.

With an expert twist of his wrist Lord Ullenwood upturned the box and the two cubes of ivory danced across the table.

'*Quatre-deuce* — six,' called Sir James

gleefully. 'Hah, Elliot, perhaps your luck is changing at last.'

The marquis smiled. 'It cannot last for ever, James.'

'I'll wager you cannot throw that again before you throw another seven,' said Lord Northby.

The marquis scooped up the dice and dropped them back into the box.

'You think not?'

With a smile he picked up the little rouleau table and tipped its contents onto the green baize. A gasp ran round the table.

'Elliot, have you lost your senses?' Sir James expostulated.

'No, James, but I grow bored.' He looked around the table. 'Does anyone care to match my stake?'

There was silence, then Lord Northby leaned forward. Slowly the old man put his hand inside his coat and pulled out a parchment document, folded and sealed.

'It's play or pay with me,' he said. 'No point in writing vowels that I can't cover, so here it is. My final bid.' He placed the document on top of the pile. 'My house and everything in it, Ullenwood.'

A murmur of surprise ran around the table. A red-faced gentleman in a puce coat shook his head in protest.

'No, my lord, you cannot — '

Lord Northby rounded on him, snarling.

'I'll do what I want in my own house, damn you.'

The marquis waited patiently until the mutterings had died down. Then he looked across the table.

'My lord, I beg you will consider before you do this.'

Lord Northby pulled himself up.

'I have considered, sir. My house and all its contents.' His lip curled. 'Mark you, Ullenwood, that means everything: my dogs, my debts, my servants — and my damned granddaughter. Will you accept?'

The two men regarded each other. The marquis's face was impassive.

'I have never yet refused a stake, my lord,' he said at last.

'Very well then. Make your play.'

The dice rattled in the leather box and danced out on to the table while the onlookers held their breath. A seven would see Lord Northby the winner, six would give the marquis everything.

'*Quatre-cinque* — nine!'

'My dear James, we are all capable of adding the numbers,' murmured the marquis, giving his friend a pained look. He picked up the dice and cast again. The little cubes left the box with some force and one bounced off the rebated table edge before coming to rest in front of Lord Northby. There was a terrible silence around the table.

'*Cinque-ace*,' said Lord Ullenwood. 'My game, I think.'

No one replied. Lord Northby gazed for some minutes at the dice, then he pushed back his chair and rose stiffly to his feet.

'Congratulations, sir.' He bowed, turned and walked slowly out of the room. As the door closed behind him the chattering began.

'Well I'll be . . . ' Sir James wiped his brow with a large red handkerchief and looked up at Lord Ullenwood.

'By Gad, Elliot I have never seen you so cool.'

The marquis was staring at the parchment, its red seal gleaming in the candlelight.

'Why should I not be?' he said slowly. '*I* had little to lose. As for Northby . . . I'll talk to him in the morning.'

'I'd say it was the brandy,' opined Sir James. 'He was drinking pretty heavily this — My God, what was that?'

'A pistol-shot,' replied the marquis.

A momentary silence had followed the loud retort but now chairs were overturned as the gentlemen jumped up and moved as one towards the door. The marquis shouldered his way through and came up to a bewildered footman standing on the landing.

'Where is Lord Northby?'

'The . . . the library sir. He's shot himself!'

* * *

A doctor was summoned, but everyone knew it was already too late. The guests returned to the saloon to revive themselves with more of the dead man's brandy while Lord Ullenwood took charge of the situation.

'And who else should do so?' demanded Mr Granthorpe. 'After all, this house is yours, now, my lord.'

Lord Ullenwood picked up the document still lying on the hazard table and broke the seal. He spread the crackling parchment on the table and studied it, frowning.

'It seems my lord had planned this: it looks very much like a will, with myself as sole beneficiary.' He sighed. 'I'll get my own man to go through it tomorrow.'

The butler came up to him, bowing.

'My lord, Miss Beaumarsh has asked if you would spare her a few moments.'

'Who the devil is Miss Beaumarsh?' demanded Sir James.

'Lord Northby's granddaughter, sir,' replied the butler woodenly.

Lord Ullenwood refolded the parchment.

'You had better look after this for me, James. I'll be back shortly.'

He followed the butler to the next floor and along a narrow corridor to a small, book-lined room. There, seated at a desk, he found a dark-haired young lady in a grey gown. She was studying a large ledger, a quill held between her ink-stained fingers. She looked so slight that at first he thought she must be a child, fifteen at the most; then she looked up and he realized his mistake. The face with its candid grey eyes that regarded him so steadily was that of a young woman. She put down her pen and rose.

'That will be all, Royd. Please leave us.'

After dismissing the butler she turned to face the marquis. She was pale but seemed perfectly composed. Her dark hair was scraped back into a tight knot at the back of her head with no ornament or ribbon. Her sober appearance struck him as entirely appropriate for the occasion.

'Miss Beaumarsh, may I say how sorry I am that we should meet in these tragic circumstances?'

'Thank you,' she said quietly. 'It was not entirely unexpected. I wondered what Grandfather would do if he lost his wager.'

'You knew what he was planning?'

'Oh yes.' She moved to a chair on one side of the empty fireplace, and gestured him to take a seat opposite. 'My grandfather informed me of it yesterday morning. He said he would either recover his fortune or lose everything.'

'Then perhaps, too, you will know why he chose *me* to take on his wager?'

Again those grey eyes met his gaze without flinching.

'Everyone knows the rich Lord Ullenwood, with his fortune, his racehorses and his . . . women. As much as Grandfather admired anyone he admired you, I think. He always said you played square.' Her dark brows lifted slightly. 'You are shocked, my lord. Perhaps you did not know Lord Northby well?'

'No, Miss Beaumarsh, I did not.'

'Then I will explain. He was eccentric, and very selfish,' she said bluntly. 'For years he has been selling off the land and gambling away his fortune. Then, last quarter day, he discovered there was nothing left save the house, a little of the estate — and me.' She sighed. 'I am — was — a sad disappointment. As Grandpapa's only relative it was incumbent upon me to redeem the family: I was to marry a fortune and provide a male heir to continue the title, but when I was presented at eighteen I did not *take*, you see. The

Northby debts are so great they overshadowed the advantages of marrying into a line that goes back to the Conqueror. And, as you can see, I am no beauty to tempt a suitor.'

'No.'

She laughed.

'You need not be quite so frank, my lord!'

'What? Oh.' In spite of the situation he found himself grinning. 'My apologies, madam, I was agreeing that your family's debts would be a disadvantage, I did not mean to insult you.'

'I believe you. But pray, tell me, what happens now?'

He frowned. 'I am not sure. I must consider the legality of that document — '

'Oh it is perfectly legitimate,' she interrupted him. 'Grandpapa called in his lawyer to draw it up: he was very pleased with the result.'

'I am very sorry,' he said. 'You are placed in a most difficult situation. I would not wish to make it worse for you.'

Again that infectious laugh. She looked truly amused.

'Lord Ullenwood, I have lived for the past five years under the thumb of a petty tyrant. I have kept house for him, made every shift possible to keep the creditors at bay and acted as his hostess when required, which was not often. What could you do to me that could be worse than that? Unless,' she added thoughtfully, 'you mean to ravish me?'

'Whatever you may have heard of me, Miss Beaumarsh. I do *not* ravish innocent young women!'

'I am glad to hear it, Lord Ullenwood.'

He looked at her sharply, wondering if she was laughing at him, but she met his fierce gaze with an innocent look.

'Very well then, madam, let us consider: is there no one you can turn to, no aunt or cousin?'

'None that I know. There may be some distant relatives, but why should they want to help me? No, I shall have to make my own way in the world. I have a little money saved: that must suffice until I can find a way to earn my living.' She rose, as if to bring the interview to a close. 'Perhaps you will give me a day or two to make my arrangements?'

He found himself saying, 'I should like you to stay on for the moment, Miss Beaumarsh. If that document is found to be legal, and I am indeed the owner here, I shall need someone to look after the house for me until I decide what to do with it, and to carry out a full inventory.'

She nodded.

'Of course. I will do my best to give

satisfaction, my lord.'

She stood before him, hands clasped, eyes lowered, but again he had the distinct impression that she was laughing at him and when he spoke it was more harshly than he had intended.

'Please remain in this room until I have sent everyone away.' Immediately he regretted his cold tone: he said gently, 'I have sent for the doctor, although there is nothing he can do for Lord Northby — would you like him to attend you when he arrives?' He took her hand. 'Perhaps he could give you something to help you rest.'

'No, sir, but thank you for your consideration. I am perfectly well.' He felt the little fingers flutter within his grasp and she said, a little self-consciously, 'Believe me, my lord, I do feel my situation quite dreadfully, but I am not one to break down easily. No doubt you find my lack of sensibility quite . . . unbecoming.'

He raised her fingers to his lips.

'On the contrary Miss Beaumarsh. After the events of the past hour, I am vastly relieved.'

* * *

Returning to the Red Saloon the marquis found most of the guests had already departed and he requested that the others should now follow suit.

'A bad business, Elliot,' said Sir James, shaking his head. 'I will call on you tomorrow — I mean, today — in case I can be of service.'

'Thank you, James. Come and take dinner with me. I am going home to sleep until then.'

Mr Granthorpe sauntered past.

'Said you had the luck of the devil, Ullenwood,' he sneered. 'Not only have you won yourself a sizeable property, but you have Northby's granddaughter thrown in — cosy little armful, is she?'

In one smooth movement the marquis turned, his right hand forming into a fist and coming up to land with devastating effect on Granthorpe's chin, sending him crashing to the floor.

'By God, sir, you'll answer for that,' gasped Granthorpe, raising himself on one elbow.

'Oh no I won't! There has been enough folly this night, without capping it with a duel. Go home and soak your head, Granthorpe.'

* * *

When Lord Ullenwood eventually departed, all traces of night had left the sky and the darkness had given way to an icy dawn. He stopped beside his carriage and looked back at the house. The unforgiving morning light showed just how run-down the building had become.

'Winner takes all,' he murmured. 'A run-down mansion, an estate that's been bled dry and a poor little dab of a girl who will need to be provided for.' He jumped into the coach. 'Damme if it doesn't make one want to give up hazard. Drive on, John!'

2

Rosamond was standing by the window on the upper landing when Lord Ullenwood's carriage turned into the drive two days later. The matched bays picked their way over the uneven surface and disappeared from view beneath the huge portico.

'Miss Rosamond, Miss Rosamond, he's here, miss!' the chambermaid's breathless voice preceded her, but soon she came clumping into sight, hauling herself up the final few steps to the landing.

'If you have come to announce that Lord Ullenwood has arrived, Meggie, I would much rather you did so in a more dignified manner,' said Rosamond, pulling her shawl more closely about her. 'Shouting up the stairs is not the accepted mode in any establishment, except perhaps a tavern.'

'Yes, miss; sorry, miss.' Meggie bobbed an ungainly curtsy and wiped her hands nervously on her apron.

Rosamond allowed herself a faint smile.

'Yes, well. You will need to remember it, Meggie, if we are to find you a position in a gentleman's household.'

'Oh, miss, do you really think we shall all be turned off?'

Rosamond was sure of it, but she did not want to upset the servants any more than was necessary so she shook her head.

'That is what I am going to find out,' was all she would reply as she left the room.

* * *

It took her several minutes to make her way down to the entrance hall, and she found the butler waiting for her at the foot of the grand staircase.

'Lord Ullenwood is waiting for you in the Red Saloon, ma'am.'

'Thank you, Royd. I think we should offer the marquis some refreshment — '

'His lordship has already requested cognac, miss, and ratafia for yourself,' said the butler, avoiding her eye. 'That is where I was going when I saw you — '

'What right — ?' Rosamond broke off, biting her tongue to prevent an unseemly outburst. She looked up. 'Then go and fetch the cognac, Royd, but no ratafia. I will drink . . . champagne.'

Royd looked slightly shocked at this, but seeing the martial light in Miss Beaumarsh's eyes he said nothing and went off to do her bidding. Rosamond crossed the hall and paused briefly to drop her thick woollen shawl on to the console table. It was a serviceable wrap, and necessary in the chilly upper rooms of the mansion. She caught sight of her reflection in the large mirror above the console table and sighed. She knew the black crêpe did not suit her; it was the gown she had worn when her parents had died several years earlier, before high-waisted gowns and diaphanous materials had become the fashion. The stiff bodice was too loose for her slight figure and made her look even more waif-like, not at all the assured woman she wanted to portray. She pinched her cheeks to try to add a little colour, and tucked a stray lock of hair behind her ear, but she knew there was nothing she could do about the dark circles under her eyes. Resolutely, she squared her shoulders and entered the Red Saloon.

* * *

Lord Ullenwood was standing by the window, looking out over the park. As she entered the room he turned.

'I am sorry if I have kept you waiting my lord.'

'No matter.' He waited until she had closed

the door behind her then said abruptly, 'There should be a footman to do that. Where is he?'

'Gone, sir.'

'Gone?'

'My grandfather turned the servants off weeks ago, when he could no longer pay them. We have only Royd, the butler, and a few housemaids.' Her chin tilted up defiantly. 'We hired the servants for that final card party.'

'The devil you did! What — ?' He broke off as a discreet scratching on the door heralded the arrival of the butler with refreshments.

Rosamond moved to a chair.

'Will you not sit down, my lord?'

The marquis chose a chair opposite and gestured to the table beside him. 'Put the tray down there: I'll deal with it.'

'Yes, his lordship will serve me, Royd, thank you.' Rosamond spoke very deliberately, reluctant to allow the marquis to control the proceedings.

As the door closed behind the servant, Lord Ullenwood gave her a quizzical look.

'Champagne, Miss Beaumarsh?'

'Yes, I will take a glass, thank you.' She smiled, deliberately misunderstanding his question.

She waited patiently while he opened the

bottle, watching the way his strong hands dealt with the cork. She cast a quick glance at his harsh features and the thought flitted across her mind that it would not be wise to provoke this man, or those lean fingers might find their way about her throat. She shook off this image and gave him another smile as he handed her a glass.

'I think before we go any further, Miss Beaumarsh, I should inform you that it is very unlikely I shall inherit this house, despite your grandfather's will.'

'I know.' She flushed a little under his harsh gaze. 'I was considering the matter, after you had left. There can be no doubt that my grandfather shot himself, and thus his estate will go to the Crown, I believe?'

'That is correct. I am sorry.' She took a sip of champagne while he continued. 'My lawyers will contest it, of course, for their are witnesses who will testify that I won the house and the estate in a wager shortly before Lord Northby's death, but I believe all must be sold to settle his debts and I would be loath to drag your grandfather's name through the courts . . . '

'No, please, let it go,' she said quickly. 'What difference does it make to me if Northby Manor belongs to you or the Crown?'

'I am very sorry, Miss Beaumarsh.'

She lifted her hand as if to ward off his sympathy.

'It matters not.'

Silence hung about them. Lord Ullenwood cleared his throat.

'I shall instruct my lawyers to do their best to delay seizure of the house. It will give us — you — a little time, but I do not hold out much hope. You had best prepare your staff for the worst.'

'They already expect it, my lord.'

'You must beware: in these cases the servants can sometimes become a little . . . careless of their master's property.' As if to illustrate the point, a shaft of morning sunlight suddenly lit the room, shining like a beacon upon a sideboard and clearly showing up two round circles in the dust. There could be no doubt that the marquis saw it. 'Have any items gone missing, Miss Beaumarsh?'

'No.' Rosamond salved her conscience by telling herself this was not a lie, since she had removed the candlesticks herself and given them to her grandfather's mistress. After all, the poor woman would get no other reward for her years of faithful service. She felt the marquis looking at her and added, 'But I will ask Royd.' She took another, larger sip from her glass. 'Perhaps you would like to see the body.'

'The body?'

'My grandfather,' she said. 'He is lying in state in the private chapel.'

'Have you arranged the funeral?'

'It is arranged for Wednesday, although I have not yet sent out the notices.'

'You need do nothing more. I will send over my man today: you may safely leave everything to him. Poor child, no wonder you are looking so drawn.'

She recoiled from his sympathy.

'I have advisers, sir.'

'Oh, who?'

'Mr Sykes — he is my grandfather's lawyer, and . . . '

'And?'

She threw him a look of dislike.

'Is that not enough? Besides, I do not have to answer to you.'

'Oh yes you do. Lord Northby entrusted you to my care.'

'That is not necessary: I am of age.'

'You told me when we last met that you have no one to turn to.'

'I did? How uncharitable of you to remember.'

'You think this an occasion for levity, Miss Beaumarsh?'

'Would you rather I collapsed in hysterics?'

Lord Ullenwood did not look pleased. He frowned at her for a moment, then stood and walked to the window.

'You also said — if you will pardon my uncharitable memory, Miss Beaumarsh — you said that you would seek a way to keep yourself.'

'Yes.' She frowned down at her hands, clasped tightly around her glass. 'Since then I have thought about it a little more, and what I should really like is to be involved in business, or — or politics: to be clerk or secretary to some gentleman of consequence.' She fixed him with a hopeful gaze. 'Perhaps you could introduce me to such a gentleman, Lord Ullenwood. My education was very good, including a fair understanding of Latin and Greek, and I read widely. I consider myself a very rational being; I am sure I would be equal to the task.'

The marquis closed his lips firmly upon the retort that sprang to mind. Instead he said gently, 'No doubt you would be equal to it, Miss Beaumarsh, but in general men have a fear of intelligent women, and distrust them when they become involved in either business or politics. You would be better advised to look for a post as a companion or governess.'

Her eyebrows went up.

'No doubt you have an aged female relative who requires someone to fetch and carry for her. Or better still, you know of a family with a nursery full of children: such a situation could keep me employed for many years.'

'I have no knowledge of any such positions,' he retorted. 'The idea of you being employed in either situation is quite hideous.'

'Then we are in agreement, my lord. But that is not the point. I must do *something*.'

'Very well then,' he said. 'You had best marry me.'

3

If Rosamond had not been sitting down at that moment, she thought she might have fainted. Certainly the world seemed to tilt alarmingly for a few moments and she could only stare up at Lord Ullenwood, wondering if she had heard him correctly.

'You look horrified at the prospect Miss Beaumarsh. Am I so repulsive?'

Hot colour flooded her cheeks.

'Horrified — no, not that, but . . . I had not expected this. Can you — do you *really* want to marry me, my lord?'

She watched as he began to pace about the room, a slight frown furrowing his brow as he sought for words.

'Miss Beaumarsh, I must marry *someone*. My family expect it, nay, they demand it of me. My wealth means that I have no need to hang out for a rich bride and since I have no one else in mind — '

Her lip curled.

'Very flattering my lord.'

He stopped in front of her and stood, staring down into her face.

'Let us have the word with no bark on it. At

the present time I am the target for every matchmaking mother, and in pursuit of a rich son-in-law some of them will go to any lengths. It is quite fatiguing to be for ever evading their tricks and stratagems. Not only that, but my family tell me it is my duty to marry and produce an heir. You called your grandfather a petty tyrant, Miss Beaumarsh, but my aunts are equally merciless in their efforts to marry me off and are constantly parading eligible females before me. You, madam, have no home, no guardian and no prospects. If you marry me you will have the first two and no need to concern yourself about the future. It will be a marriage of convenience, concluded for purely logical reasons. There will be no need for us to live in each other's pockets. We will, of course, be expected to be seen together occasionally, but once you have provided me with an heir we can each go our own way, as long as there is discretion.'

Rosamond looked down at her hands. One of the biggest prizes on the marriage mart was standing before her, offering to make her his bride. She considered the advantages. He was very rich and handsome — if one liked dark eyes that seemed to be able to look into one's soul and hair as black as a raven's wing. Disadvantages: he was arrogant, but her grandfather had been the same, so that did not overly concern her. She could think of only one serious disadvantage.

She said in a small voice, 'What if you should fall in love, my lord?'

He gave a harsh laugh.

'The women I favour are not the sort to become Lady Ullenwood. And at my age I am unlikely to succumb to a grand passion.'

'So stricken in years as you are,' she murmured, and earned another searching look from the marquis.

'At one-and-thirty I consider myself beyond the age for such nonsense,' he said stiffly. 'Now, what do you say?'

Rosamond decided to try to stand up. Her legs felt normal so she walked over to the window, looking out at the neglected water garden. She wondered if the grounds of Lord Ullenwood's houses would be in good order. She guessed they would be immaculate.

'Would I have the running of your household, sir?'

'Of course.'

She turned.

'And if, for instance, I wanted to plant a garden?'

He looked surprised.

'That might not be possible at the town house, but all the other houses have sizeable gardens, including Leverhill, my family home in Wiltshire: I am sure if you wanted to make changes that could be discussed. Although I would never agree to you cutting down all my trees, or moving a village to suit your whim.'

'I would never do such a thing. But I must have a role. I must be active.'

'Then my steward will welcome you with open arms.'

He smiled and Rosamond was taken aback by the transformation. She had heard Lord Ullenwood described as being dangerously attractive: now for the first time she thought that perhaps it was not just his wealth that made him so. She struggled to concentrate on what he was saying to her.

'Miss Beaumarsh, many couples begin marriage with no more knowledge of each other than this. Will you do me the honour of becoming my wife?'

She drew a breath.

'Thank you my lord, but I think not. It has never been my wish to be a rich man's wife, an ornament to be dressed and put on display with his other possessions. I do not believe that women are only fit to be wives and mothers — Rousseau is wrong about that!'

'Ah,' he said softly. 'I see the influence of the Wollstonecraft woman at work here.'

She put up her chin and regarded him with

a hint of defiance.

'And what of it?'

'Nothing. I believe the lady put forward some sound and reasoned arguments for greater freedom for your sex.'

'Then you must see why I would like to make my own way in the world,' she said eagerly. She gave a little sigh. 'I have considered earning my living from my pen, in the manner of Miss Burney, or the learned Miss Elizabeth Carter, but I do not have the talent for it. However, I have been well educated and see no reason why I should not be of use to some busy man.'

Miss Beaumarsh, what you seek is impossible, unless you mean to marry such a man.'

She waved an impatient hand.

'I do not see the need to marry: I could be his private secretary, attend political dinners, write his speeches — '

'It cannot be,' he interrupted her. 'Society would not call you his secretary, but something far less elegant.'

'Then Society would be at fault!'

'No doubt, but it is the world we live in.' He gave her a faint smile. 'Even Mary Wollstonecraft found it expedient to marry.'

'Do you refer to the American she met while in Paris? I agree that the dangers she faced there made it necessary for her to take a husband.'

'And the second time, when she married Mr Godwin?'

She paused, wrinkling her brow while she considered the matter.

'*That* was a marriage of minds, I think,' she said slowly. 'They came as equals to the partnership. Most couples are not so fortunate.'

'Most do not seek perfection. Come, madam: consider well before you refuse me.'

She heard the note of impatience in his voice, and decided it would be unwise to pursue the argument. Instead, she said, 'Marriage is a big step, my lord, and although I am very conscious of the honour you do me by your offer, it would be wrong of me to make a decision without some deliberation. Will you allow me a little time to consider?'

'Of course, but I would not have the world think you are unprotected now your grandfather is gone. I shall make it known that you have been left to my care, and I will find a suitable companion to come and stay with you.'

'That is not necessary, Lord Ullenwood.'

'It is very necessary, if you are not to appear an eccentric.'

'Then allow me to find my own companion.'

'Do you have someone in mind?'

She avoided his gaze.

'I will advertise.'

'And have all the scaff and raff of London at your door? No, madam, you will allow me to have my way in this.'

'You will leave me with nothing to do.'

'On the contrary, you will oblige me by producing an inventory of Lord Northby's possessions. It must be done, and as soon as possible. My own lawyer will consult with Mr Sykes and between them they will advise you of what you may legitimately consider your own.'

She moved away from the window, looking around her.

'Very little, I suspect.'

'You may well be right.' He came towards her. 'I must go.' He took her hand, saying gently, 'Do not let your present situation overset you. Even if you decide you cannot marry me I shall not let you starve, you know.'

His sudden kindness pierced her carefully erected defences and tears pricked at her eyelids.

'It would sit ill with your reputation if you did so, my lord,' she replied gruffly.

A disturbing twinkle gleamed in his dark eyes.

'Aye,' he murmured, squeezing her fingers. 'So it would.'

A moment later he was gone. Rosamond ran to the window and waited until she saw him coming out of the house, pressing his curly brimmed beaver over his dark hair and barking a word of command to his coachman before jumping into the carriage. Rosamond was surprised at the sharp stab of disappointment she felt when he did not look back.

4

For the second time in a week Lord Ullenwood drove away from Northby Manor in a state of mild shock. What had possessed him to offer marriage to the chit? Most likely the fact that he had only that morning received another letter from his aunt Morpeth reminding him that it was time he took a wife, and that she had just the lady in mind. Miss Beaumarsh's reluctance to consider the offer had surprised him at first, but the more he thought of it the more he approved of her caution: it showed a reflective nature. Miss Beaumarsh was not one to act on impulse, and that was an asset in a wife. Perhaps she would not marry him: he found it mattered to him very little, except that if she were to become his wife, his aunts would have no occasion to nag him further!

'It's persecution, dear boy,' declared Sir James Ashby, when Elliot told him of the latest letter. 'Damme, you should tell those plaguey women to stop pestering you.'

They were dining together at Ullenwood House, and with the covers removed only the butler was in attendance, but even so the marquis did not reply until Johnson had left the room.

'I can see their point,' murmured Elliot. 'If I do not produce an heir the title will die out. I acquit my aunts of self-interest in this; they are merely concerned for the family name.'

'Well 'tis *your* name, not theirs, so you can tell 'em to go to the devil!'

Sir James had broached his second bottle and was in belligerent mood.

'That's just it,' the marquis complained mildly, 'I *have* told them, but they consider it their duty to continue to — ah — advise me.'

'Damnation!' Sir James sat back in his chair and regarded his host in bewilderment. 'Damme if I understand it, Elliot. You are a ruthless devil at the card-table; there isn't a horse that you cannot master and you have killed your man in a duel on more than one occasion that I know of, and yet you cannot be rid of a pack of women!'

The marquis gave him a wry grin.

'I know. I am surprised you do not give me the cut direct.'

Sir James muttered something inarticulate and helped himself to another glass of brandy. Silence settled over the room, broken only by the crackling of the fire that blazed in the marble fireplace.

'So you went to see Northby's granddaughter today,' said Sir James at last. 'How did you find her?'

'Remarkably calm, given the events of Friday night.'

'Hmm.' Sir James scowled into his glass. 'A rum business, to leave the gel to your care.'

'Yes, I thought so, too.'

'What are you going to do with her? Perhaps one of your aunts could be of some use and take her in.'

'Perhaps. I was thinking of marriage.'

'Marrying her off, you mean?' said Sir James, lifting his glass to his lips. 'Good idea. Do you have anyone in mind?'

'I thought I might marry her myself.'

The marquis smiled as Sir James spluttered and began to cough violently.

'Dear, dear, Ashby: surely my brandy is not that bad?' he murmured.

Sir James threw him a reproachful glance.

'Damn you, Ullenwood, 'twas your funning that made me choke!'

'Oh, but I am serious, my friend. Northby's chit has an excellent lineage — I have already made enquiries about that. Northby's daughter married a gentleman, but there was no money, which naturally did not please her father. It seems Northby would have nothing to do with them, although he did pay for the girl's education and took the chit in when the parents died. From my dealings with her she seems a sensible little thing. And marriage to her would put an end to the barracking of my family at very little inconvenience to myself. She has been used to running Northby's establishment so I have no doubt she could run my houses. It seems an admirable arrangement.'

Sir James stared at him.

'And has she agreed to this?'

'No, but I think she will. However, I would be obliged if you would not spread it around just yet.'

'No, of course not. But — Elliot, surely you haven't developed a *tendre* for the girl?'

'After two meetings? Do be sensible, James. No, *I* need a wife; *she* needs a home.'

'I've only seen the girl once, and she didn't look your type, old friend. I mean, she's no beauty.'

'True, but she's well enough. And in my experience it is not a good thing to have an attractive wife; the husband is forever fighting off men who want to seduce her.'

'Men such as yourself, perhaps,' said Sir James.

'No, no, you wrong me,' said the marquis smoothly. 'I have never seduced a married woman. It has never been necessary.'

'Meaning they fall all too readily at your feet! 'Fore Gad you are a lucky devil, Ullenwood!'

The marquis raised his glass and smiled sweetly at his friend.

'Yes,' he said softly. 'I think I am.'

5

The following morning Royd came to Rosamond's room to announce that a Mrs Tomlinson had called, and was wishful to see her.

'She brought this letter for you, miss,' he added, holding out a small silver tray.

Rosamond took the paper and unfolded it. The heavy black writing was unfamiliar, but she guessed immediately that it was from Lord Ullenwood. She scanned the note quickly.

> *I am sorry that I cannot come in person to present my cousin to you. She is a widow, and free to bear you company, if you will agree to it. Yours, etc, Ullenwood.*

'Short and terse, as I would expect from him,' she muttered. 'Well, Royd, where is she?'

'I left her in the library, miss.'

She rose. 'Then I had best see what sort of female he wants to thrust upon me.'

* * *

Rosamond entered the library, expecting to find a little old lady awaiting her. Instead she found herself face to face with a young woman not much older than herself. Mrs Tomlinson was dressed in a fur-lined pelisse of dove grey and a modish bonnet that covered most of her hair, although a few golden curls were visible. As Rosamond hesitated in the doorway, the lady came forward, her generous mouth curving into a wide smile and her green eyes positively twinkling with merriment.

'Miss Beaumarsh, how good of you to receive me. I begged Elliot to wait until he could come with me, but you know what he is like; once he gets a maggot into his head nothing will shift him, and it is much easier to do as he wishes than to argue with him. I am sure you are wishing me at the very devil.'

'Not at all,' murmured Rosamond, bemused.

'Well, you are a good deal too kind. What has Elliot told you of me? Nothing? If that is not just like him!'

Rosamond managed a faint smile.

'Will you not be seated, ma'am?'

'Thank you, and please, call me Arabella.' Mrs Tomlinson sank onto a sofa in a cloud of grey velvet. 'Now, you will want to know all about me.'

'I think first I would like to know what

Lord Ullenwood has told you about *me*,' said Rosamond.

'Very little, the wretch!' returned the widow, with another of her warm smiles. 'He said you had been left to his care, and since it would not be at all the thing for him to take you into his bachelor household, for the moment he must provide you with a suitable chaperon. So he asked me to come along and visit you, to see if we should suit.'

'Did he also tell you that my grandfather died very recently? My period of mourning is only just beginning. Forgive me, but I cannot think that such a quiet existence as I lead would suit you.

'No of course not, if I was expected to stay with you for the full term of your mourning, but Elliot says it will be for no more than a month.'

'Oh, and how can he be so sure about that?' said Rosamond, bridling.

Mrs Tomlinson shook her head.

'I do not know. Mayhap he thinks that will be long enough for you to decide what you wish to do.'

'I am not sure that my *wishes* will count for very much,' sighed Rosamond. 'You see, I have no money and must earn my living as best I can.'

'But I thought you were Elliot's ward.'

Rosamond looked a little uncomfortable.

'My grandfather consigned me to his care,' she said. 'There is no legal obligation, and I should not wish to be a burden upon Lord Ullenwood. Therefore, I must find employment.'

Mrs Tomlinson regarded her with awe.

'Must you? How do you propose to do that?'

'I am not sure,' came the pensive reply. 'I had hoped someone might employ me in a clerical capacity. You see I have looked after the household here for years compiling the accounts, reading all the letters and writing the replies.'

'But Lord Northby was your grandfather,' Mrs Tomlinson pointed out. 'Other men may have . . . secrets, matters that they would rather not share with a female.'

'Do you refer to their amorous adventures?' asked Rosamond, unmoved. 'I had thought of that, and I consider it would be much easier for me, as a female, to deal with their mistresses.'

The widow clapped her hands to her mouth, her eyes twinkling merrily.

'Miss Beaumarsh, I am deeply shocked!'

'You are? Then I am sorry for it,' replied Rosamund, an answering gleam in her own eyes. 'I have been used to looking after my grandfather's mistress for years. She lived in the east wing, you see, so there was no avoiding her. In fact, we became very good friends, and I miss her dreadfully, but when my grandfather died she insisted that she must leave the Manor and she has forbidden me to visit her.' She sighed. 'However, I can see that some gentlemen might find it disconcerting to discuss such things with me.'

'A governess is considered a genteel occupation,' offered Mrs Tomlinson.

Rosamond grimaced

'Yes, but in most cases the position is that of a drudge. It is the same with a lady's companion. I *could* seek a post as a teacher, perhaps, although the minor increase in independence would be tempered by the fact that I should be looking after dozens of children at a time, rather than one or two — *not* a pleasant thought!' She sighed. 'My education has made me useful for little else, except to be a housekeeper, which is what I have been in all but name for the past year, since Grandpapa decided we must cut down on our expenditure and turned off most of the servants. So, perhaps, I should look for such a position. At least housekeepers seem to have some measure of independence.'

'But what of marriage, have you no thought of getting a husband?'

Decisively, Rosamond shook her head.

'I see marriage as another form of slavery.' She flushed. 'Oh, I am sorry, ma'am. I did not mean to be insensitive!'

'No, no, I am not at all offended. Everyone knows that my marriage was arranged to bring two properties together, and all in all it worked out very well. Dear Tommy was very kind to me, and I was very fond of him. Unfortunately he died before I could give him an heir. Drowned while out sailing,' she added, a shadow of unhappiness momentarily clouding her eyes.

'I am very sorry.'

'Yes, so too am I, but I do not repine. He left me with a very handsome allowance, you see, and I have found that being a widow can be very amusing; only I am afraid I was too indiscreet and Elliot packed me off to live with Mama until the scandal was forgotten. Very high-handed of him, of course, and unfair, too! No one raises any objection to his having a mistress, and that is far more indecent than my little flirtations. Oh, I am sorry; I should not talk so in front of you.'

'You need not worry. As you have said, Lord Ullenwood's affairs are common knowledge.'

'Well, he does not flaunt his women before the *ton*, but he is so rich that all the world wants to know what he is about,' returned Arabella, frankly. 'And his latest flirt — Barbara Lythmore — she must be costing him a pretty penny, for everyone knows that he owns her house in Clarges Street and, if the gossips are correct, he has bought her the very handsome carriage that she is seen driving about the park each day. It is pulled by the prettiest little cream ponies, and I am quite *sick* with envy!' Arabella frowned for a moment, considering the matter, then her brow cleared. She smiled, and said brightly, 'And then Elliot wrote to Mama and said he had need of me to keep you company, if you would have me, which makes me think of him as quite my favourite cousin again. So you see, Miss Beaumarsh, if you let me stay here with you, it will be the very thing for both of us.' She cast a beseeching look at Rosamond. 'Do say you will let me come.'

Rosamond smiled.

'I think I should like to have you live with me, Arabella. I should like that very much!'

6

By the next afternoon Mrs Tomlinson was in residence and Rosamond was surprised at how much more comfortable she felt with a female companion in the house. However, during the next few days she was too busy to think of anything save the immediate business of her grandfather's funeral. Lord Ullenwood's secretary had taken over the arrangements, but the household had to be put into mourning, accounts to be paid and there were visitors who must be seen: friends of Lord Northby who came to pay their condolences, although the manner of his death kept the majority of his acquaintance away. The funeral itself was a quiet affair, with Lord Northby's remains being interred within the private chapel, despite the uncharitable opinion of the few who were scandalized that a suicide should be given a Christian burial. It was a bitterly cold day and from the window of the Red Saloon Rosamond watched as a pitifully small number of gentlemen made their way to the chapel, heads bent against the icy wind and sleet that blew relentlessly across the park.

She had arranged for refreshments to be served after the interment, and had to endure several hours of embarrassed and stilted conversation. Mrs Tomlinson proved a great help, stepping into the breach when Rosamond was unable to find words to reply to some well-meaning comment. Earlier in the day there had been a painful interview with Mr Sykes, the family lawyer, who told her that Lord Northby's suicide made the reading of the will irrelevant, since all his possessions would be claimed by the Crown. It was no more than she had expected, but still it weighed heavily upon her spirits, compounded by the anxiety of what was to become of her. She had seen little of Lord Ullenwood. He attended the funeral, but came to take his leave after a short time, assuring her that he would call again in a day or two.

'You have my cousin to bear you company, and the lawyers are doing all they can to delay the confiscation of the property by the courts.'

'So you are leaving now.' It was all she could think to say as she gave him her hand.

'There is no reason for me to stay. Indeed, to do so could even give rise to conjecture.' He squeezed her fingers and gave her the ghost of a smile. 'Try not to be anxious. I shall not let anything terrible happen to you.'

'No, of course not,' she said, but once he had left the room she felt unaccountably bereft of support.

* * *

Rosamond was busy in the library the next morning when Lord Ullenwood was shown in.

'I was afraid I might find you still at breakfast,' he said, stripping off his gloves as he advanced into the room.

'Not at all, my lord.' She indicated the papers on the desk. 'I told you I like to keep busy, and have made a start on the inventory. Most of Grandfather's books are already catalogued, but the pictures and furniture must be itemized.' She pulled off her linen apron and tossed it onto the desk. 'Will you not be seated, sir?'

He chose a chair by the window, where the early morning sun gleamed on his black hair.

'Where is my cousin?'

Rosamond could not suppress a smile.

'She is not such an early riser as I am. I suspect she is even now sipping at her chocolate.'

He frowned.

'She should be here to chaperon you.'

'That is hardly necessary.'

'Not with me, perhaps, but if you have other visitors — '

'My grandfather did not encourage visitors,' she told him, 'but be assured, sir, if it had been anyone but yourself I have no doubt that Royd would have denied me, knowing I am alone. Which reminds me, why did you tell your cousin that she would be here no more than a month?'

'One of my aunts is coming to stay with me at the beginning of March, and once she is here it will be perfectly acceptable for you to move into Ullenwood House.'

Rosamond stiffened.

'You assume a great deal, sir. I have not agreed to that.'

'You were left to my care, madam.'

'Yes, but I am still anxious to find a way to support myself.'

'After our previous discussions I thought we had agreed that marriage was the only solution.'

'Not at all,' she retorted, sitting very straight in her chair. 'I have not yet fully investigated the alternatives.' Her eyes narrowed. 'Why do you smile at me in that smug way? Doubtless you think I should accept your proposal and consider myself fortunate in the extreme. Let me assure you that I am far from agreeing with you on that!'

'Good God, woman, do not fly up into the boughs merely because of a look! True, I do think marriage to me is the best solution for you — I confess if you tell me you would prefer the life of a governess it would be a serious blow to my self-esteem.'

She gave a reluctant smile.

'Then I shall not say it, and apologize for losing my temper, sir, but pray do not rush me: I am sure there must be another solution, one that does not involve such a sacrifice on your part.'

'I have already explained to you that I would not consider it a sacrifice, but you do not need to give me your answer immediately. Bella shall stay here with you for the next few weeks and, once my aunt arrives, if you are still of the same mind, you can come to Ullenwood House as my ward, nothing more.'

'Thank you, my lord. You are very good.'

'Very well, now let us to business. From what I now know of your grandfather's affairs there is very little money left to settle with tradesmen and pay the servants.'

'As I could have told you, Lord Ullenwood, had you asked me. I have been looking after the accounts here for some time.'

He ignored her angry tone.

'Then perhaps you will advise me precisely

what you require to settle matters here at the end of the month.' He pulled a roll of notes from his coat pocket and handed them to her. 'That should be enough there to settle any immediate bills, and to buy yourself some new mourning clothes.'

'Th-thank you,' she stammered. 'But there is not the least need — '

'Oh I think there is. Bella will not allow you to go about in such outmoded fashions!'

Rosamond flinched. It was an unpleasant feeling to know Lord Ullenwood considered her a dowd. As soon as he had left she went into the Red Saloon and walked over to a large mirror placed between the long windows. A very dejected figure stared back at her. Her hair was scraped back from her sallow face and a shapeless black crêpe gown hung from her shoulders. She had been rather a plump young girl of fifteen when her parents had died: eight years later the puppy fat had gone, and although it had been a simple matter to let down the hem of her old mourning gown she had not considered it necessary to take it in. After all, there was no one to notice. But the marquis *had* noticed, and Rosamond was ashamed that she should appear before him so careless of her appearance. She straightened her shoulders: whatever her fate, she would achieve nothing looking such a fright and she determined to do something about it.

* * *

Later that day Rosamond invited Mrs Tomlinson to her bedchamber, where she had spread all her mourning clothes across the bed.

'They are all far too big for me,' she confided, 'but I should like to know which ones you think could be suitably altered to fit? Lord Ullenwood has left me some money . . . '

She trailed off and waited anxiously as the widow surveyed the gowns, their varying shades of black and grey billowing over the bed like a dense storm-cloud. After a moment Arabella stepped forward and swept them all on to the floor.

'You must have new,' she said decidedly. 'How much has Elliot given you?'

Rosamond told her. Arabella snorted.

'Not enough. If anyone should know the cost of a woman's wardrobe it is Ullenwood; his mistresses are amongst the best turned-out women in Town. Come. We must make a list of everything that is needed and then I shall take you to visit my own dressmaker.'

'She could make me one gown, I suppose,'

said Rosamond, following her out of the room. 'As to the rest, I must be economical.'

'I will not hear of it,' retorted Arabella. 'We shall buy you everything that is the best. You are Lord Ullenwood's ward now and must look the part.'

'Then I must apply to the marquis for further funds.'

'Not at all. When Tommy died he left me a very generous settlement.'

Rosamond stopped.

'But I cannot allow you to pay for my clothes!'

Mrs Tomlinson had reached the foot of the stairs, but now she stopped and turned to look up at Rosamond, her green eyes wide.

'But why not? I have so many clothes I cannot possibly buy more at present, and it will be so entertaining to have the dressing of you.'

⋆ ⋆ ⋆

Thus it was that over the next few days Lord Northby's ancient dress chariot was to be seen standing outside the most fashionable shops in Bond Street, Pall Mall and Covent Garden. Soon Rosamond's head was spinning as a succession of plain gowns and pelisses were ordered and various rolls of bombazine, muslin and linen laid out for her approval. She stood by, mute, as Bella ordered crêpe hoods, chamois shoes and gloves ('very dull, my dear, and therefore perfect for mourning!') plus a bewildering assortment of shawls, fans and handkerchiefs.

'Well, another very satisfactory day's work!' declared Mrs Tomlinson when they were once more seated in the chariot and on their way back to Northby House.

Rosamond looked at the various packages stacked around them.

'I cannot think that I shall need all this. And I have no idea how much everything will cost.'

'And nor should you,' said Bella. 'You are in mourning for your grandfather and should not have to worry your head with such trivialities.' She took out her crumpled list and studied it. 'Now, we have the muslin skirt that you can wear immediately, and Madame has promised that the undress of Norwich crêpe will be delivered tomorrow together with the fur-lined pelisse and hood that you will need for walking out. Then, there are the two day and evening gowns, and the black silk to be delivered later. Of course, you will not require the silk until you are out of your first period of deep mourning, but the grey silk will be suitable for you to wear on informal occasions, or when we are dining alone. Hmm, reticules, gloves, fans . . . what have we forgotten?'

'Nothing, I am sure, Bella! I have never had so many new things at one time.'

'No, that is quite apparent,' retorted Mrs Tomlinson. 'I know one should not speak ill of the dead, but it was quite *monstrous* of Lord Northby to keep you hidden away so.'

'But I did not object, Bella. In fact, I was quite happy to live retired, especially after my disastrous presentation. The lady Grandpapa brought in to take me to all those parties was very kind, but when she found I was such an awkward, tongue-tied dab of a girl she quite despaired of me.'

'Well I do not despair of you,' declared Arabella. 'Once we have you in your new gowns and my coiffeuse has cut your hair and rearranged it more becomingly, I think you will look very well. Besides, you are no longer a shy child of eighteen but a sensible lady of three-and-twenty, and I think you will cut a dash in any company — oh, now I remember! You do not have a black parasol.'

Rosamond giggled.

'But it is February!'

'Nevertheless, you will need one when Elliot takes you driving in the park.'

'Oh, will he take me driving, then?'

'Not a doubt of it. He is a famous whip, always to be seen driving himself around Town.'

Rosamond frowned at the parcels piled upon the seat.

'Does . . . does he take his mistress driving in the park?' she asked tentatively.

'Oh no, he is far too discreet for that. Mrs Lythmore likes to keep up the pretence of being a respectable widow.'

'But perhaps she is. You should not malign her without knowing the truth.'

Arabella laughed at her.

'My dear Rosamond, everyone in Town knows it is the truth! Lythmore left her very well provided for, but she soon ran through her money and was obliged to find a protector. Elliot is only the latest of them!' She sat back against the well-padded seat and regarded Rosamond with a little smile. 'But let us not talk of Elliot, for we are having such an enjoyable day shopping, are we not? What a pity we forgot the parasol, but it does not matter, I am sure we will think of several other things we shall need and we can purchase them all the next time.'

'There will be no next time! I shall never go shopping again!' cried Rosamond, throwing up her hands.

'Oh, but — ' Bella observed the twinkle in

her companion's eyes and broke off, chuckling. 'Now you are joking me! Only wait until you have put on your new clothes and see how much better you feel.'

* * *

Rosamond was not convinced, but when the coiffeuse engaged by Mrs Tomlinson had called upon her, she put on one of her new gowns and went in search of Arabella. She found her in the Red Saloon, strumming idly on the pianoforte.

'Well, Bella,' she said shyly, 'what do you think?' She stood before the mirror, frowning at her reflection.

Mrs Tomlinson came to stand beside her and placed her hands on her shoulders.

'I should almost say you are a different being,' she declared. 'I knew the Norwich crêpe would look well on you.'

Rosamond looked at herself: the high-waisted grey gown fell in soft folds about her, making her look much taller. It was the most fashionable of the dresses Bella had chosen for her, but the heavy material was warm and comforting in such a large, draughty house.

'Celestine has worked wonders with your hair,' commented Bella.

Rosamond nodded and gazed in wonder at

the new style. Most of her heavy dark hair was drawn up into a softly coiled topknot, banded with a black silk ribbon, while small tendrils curled softly against her forehead and cheeks. Bella was right, she thought. She looked like a different person — she even felt like a different person.

A clanging of the doorbell could be heard in the distance and moments later the butler came in to announce Lord Ullenwood.

The ladies looked at one another. Rosamond cleared her throat.

'Show him in, Royd.' She glanced at her friend. 'Do you think he will notice?'

'If he does not I shall call a doctor to him immediately,' retorted Arabella, smiling.

Rosamond swallowed nervously and moved across the room to stand before the fireplace, trying not to fidget as the door opened and the marquis was announced. He stepped forward and bowed.

'Good day to you, Miss Beaumarsh, Cousin, I . . . ' His words died away as he straightened and his eyes came to rest for the first time upon Miss Beaumarsh.

Her nervousness disappeared, replaced by amusement as she saw the shock and surprise in his face. It was gone in a moment, and he raised his quizzing glass to look at her. Arabella could contain herself no longer.

'Well, Cousin, what do you think of your ward now?

The marquis allowed his gaze to move slowly over Rosamond, from her glossy topknot, past the fringed shawl and soft worsted gown that wrapped about her slender figure and down to the shoes of black chamois that peeped out from the hem of her gown. He lowered his glass.

'A transformation,' he murmured. His eyes were drawn back to her grey ones, huge and dark against her flawless pale skin. Such a look would evoke sympathy from the stoniest heart. Then he saw the gleam of amusement in her face, and found himself smiling at her.

'Well, Elliot?' demanded Arabella. 'Is she not looking well?'

'Very well, Bella. You are to be congratulated.'

'Well, thank you, but it was not all my work, you know: Rose has excellent taste.'

Rosamond flushed at that.

'Will you not be seated, my lord — in fact,' she hesitated, 'we dine in an hour, sir: would you care to join us?'

Lord Ullenwood had planned to dine at his club, but now he decided his friends could do without him.

'Thank you, Miss Beaumarsh. I shall be delighted to accept your invitation.'

Arabella cast a quick, shrewd glance at her cousin and rose from her seat.

'No need to ring the bell, Rose, I will go and find Royd and tell him to set another place.' She hurried away, leaving Rosamond to entertain the marquis.

Rosamond moved to a vacant sofa.

'I — um — do you have business you wish to discuss with me, my lord?'

'Yes.' He came across to sit beside her. 'I wanted to tell you that the lawyers will be calling tomorrow to collect the inventory.'

She gave a gasp, her hands clasped nervously in her lap.

'But it is not yet finished.'

'I know, and I am sorry for it, but my man believes the courts will want to take possession of the house and its contents within the next few days. I am sorry. I did all I could to prevent this.'

'Thank you, I am sure you did, but my grandfather's suicide made the outcome inevitable.' She gave him a shaky smile. 'One thing he did not account for in his grand plan.'

He reached over and took her hands between his own, holding them in a firm, comforting clasp.

'Rosamond — '

He saw the sudden look of fear in her eyes

and released her. Immediately she jumped up.

'There is not so very much to do to complete the inventory. The principal rooms are done, it is merely the attics, and if we make an early start I am sure we can have it complete. Ah, here is Bella come back. Well, have you seen Royd?'

'Yes it is all arranged for an extra cover to be laid for dinner,' said Arabella. She turned to the marquis. 'You are fortunate, Cos. We have rabbit tonight, and more than enough for the two of us, else Cook would have been pouring curses upon your head!'

Lord Ullenwood rose.

'Heaven forbid that I should offend your cook,' he said lightly.

'It seems the lawyers will be calling upon us tomorrow, Bella. I have explained to Lord Ullenwood that our inventory is not yet finished.'

'It is no matter,' he said. 'They will help you to finish the lists. My main concern is that you should identify what belongs to you, personally, Miss Beaumarsh.'

'Good heavens, are we to be turned out onto the street?' cried Arabella, sinking onto a chair.

'Not quite that,' responded the marquis. 'However, my man has failed to achieve any additional delay and warns that the bailiffs will descend upon you any day now. He suggests you should remove any of your personal effects tomorrow. I will send a couple of men over with a carriage to assist you — you may send anything you wish to keep to me.'

Rosamond nodded, pale but perfectly calm.

'And how long can I — can we remain here?'

'I expect them to give you notice to quit within the next few days.'

'So soon, with his lordship not yet cold in his grave? That is outrageous.'

Lord Ullenwood shook his head.

'The courts are implacable, Bella. I have no power to stop it.'

'But — '

Rosamond put up her hand.

'No, Bella, you must not rail at your cousin. He has done his best for me, I am sure. It is the law, and we will be ready to leave when word comes.'

'Thank you,' said the marquis. 'I will of course have rooms prepared for you at Ullenwood House. Unfortunately my aunt, Lady Padiham, cannot come to me sooner so you, Bella, must act as chaperon until she arrives.'

'With pleasure — I would not leave Rosamond now for anything, we have become such good friends! But, heaven and earth! How did you persuade Aunt Padiham to act as your hostess? You should know, Rosamond, that my aunt is so indolent she can never be persuaded out of her house by normal means. So, Elliot, how did you do it?'

The marquis grinned.

'I am her favourite nephew, did you not know?'

'That may be so, but I do not believe that would sway her.'

'Perhaps it is the fact that her own house is in urgent need of repair,' he said, a decided twinkle in his eyes. 'I persuaded her that it would be less trouble for her to come to me than to rent a property. However, not even my powers of persuasion could make her come to me before the end of the month, which is why I need you, Bella.'

Arabella looked at him.

'You want me to play propriety?'

His lips twitched.

'The role will have the charm of novelty for you,' he murmured.

Arabella gave a gurgle of laughter.

'For shame, Elliot, you will make dear Rose think me a hoyden.'

'And so you are, Bella, but while Miss

Beaumarsh is in deep mourning your opportunities for mischief will be few.'

'And now Rosamond is looking at me askance, and wondering what I have done to earn such a reputation,' cried the widow merrily. 'Nothing more serious than to conduct a little dalliance.'

'With Tomlinson dead less than six months,' added the marquis.

Arabella pouted.

'But if it had been anyone other than Harry Granthorpe I have no doubt you would not have been so swift to censure me!' she said.

'I should not allow you to ruin yourself with anyone, Bella. The fact that it was Granthorpe merely made it imperative that I step in to protect you. The man's a wastrel.'

'Yes, there is that,' agreed Arabella, sighing. She turned to Rosamond. 'Do you know Harry Granthorpe, my dear?'

'Yes. He was used to call upon my grandfather. I met him once or twice, but Grandpapa was careful to keep him away from me.'

'Very wise,' nodded Bella. 'He's a handsome scoundrel, but one meets him everywhere. That was why Mama insisted on carrying me off to the country.' She gave a mischievous little smile. 'I was beginning to go out of my mind with boredom at home, then dear Elliot sent me word that I was needed here.' She put out a hand and Rosamond took it, smiling.

'And I am very glad you could come to me,' she said. 'You must know, my lord, that Arabella and I are now fast friends.'

'Then I hope a little of your good sense will brush off on her.'

The widow protested hotly until Rosamond put up her hands.

'I have no doubt Lord Ullenwood is teasing you, Bella. It is very reprehensible, but you will have the opportunity to prove him wrong over the next few weeks, while you look after me.' She rose. 'Shall we go in to dinner?'

7

With so much to think about, Rosamond was happy to allow the marquis and his cousin to make most of the conversation during dinner. Despite her preoccupation, she was amused to listen to their good-natured banter and soon realized that Bella was very fond of her cousin, and relied heavily upon his judgement. After the confined existence she had known with her grandfather, where she had been allowed to meet very few of his friends, she found the thrust and parry of their conversation entertaining. She would have liked to join in, but shyness held her back. Arabella noticed how silent her friend was and did her best to include her in the conversation. When the covers were removed, and a dish of sweetmeats placed on the table, she said suddenly,

'Did you not tell me you speak French very well, Rosamond?'

'I used to be fluent, but I have not used it for some years now.'

'You must know, Rosamond, that Elliot owned a vast estate in France.'

'You exaggerate, Bella,' the marquis corrected

her. 'A large house with sizeable estates, and several farms. There is French blood in my family, you know. My father took me to visit Château Ullenwood when I was a child.'

'And can it still be in your possession?' asked Rosamond, puzzled. 'Surely such properties were lost during the long wars, or if not then, during the Terror.'

'That is what we thought, Miss Beaumarsh, but a couple of years ago I was contacted by a lawyer from Paris, who claimed to have papers proving that the estates were still legally mine. Of course, as soon as the Peace was signed last year I sent my agent to seek out this lawyer. Since then the matter has been dragging through the French courts, who are in no way minded to hurry matters.'

'Perhaps Rosamond could help you with your affairs in France, Cousin,' put in Arabella.

Rosamond shook her head.

'I am sure the marquis has very expert help in that quarter.' She turned to him. 'I imagine the courts of France are reluctant to admit that an Englishman owns even a cupful of French soil.'

'You are very right, Miss Beaumarsh. I go through the procedures for form's sake, but I have little hope that anything will come of it.'

'Could you not go to France yourself?' she

asked. 'Would that not give weight to your claim?'

'Perhaps, but it would also give weight to Bonaparte and his government, which I am loath to do.'

'Lord yes,' agreed Arabella, wrinkling her nose in distaste. 'You would have to make your bow at court, to the very people who executed the poor king and queen so barbarically.'

'Mr Fox and his followers were very quick to visit Paris last year, as soon as the Treaty was signed,' murmured Rosamond, selecting a sweetmeat from the silver dish.

The marquis nodded. 'They support the Peace.'

'And you do not?' Rosamond's dark brows lifted. 'Surely you agree that it gives Addington and the government the opportunity to recoup a little. We have been at war for so long, and it is a costly business.'

The marquis refilled his wine glass.

'True,' he said, 'but peace comes at a price. We have given up Egypt, and the Cape, yet Bonaparte uses his influence to prevent Italy and Holland from trading with us. Do you truly believe such a peace can last? France is determined to block our trade while continuing her own expansion.'

Rosamond sighed. 'No, you are right, although I am sorry for it.'

‘Poor Rose, you sound very downcast, and that is not at all like you,’ put in Arabella. ‘No doubt you are melancholy at the thought of leaving your home.’

Rosamond was quick to disclaim.

‘I fear I am out of practice at making myself agreeable in company. I assure you I am not unhappy.’

‘But surely you must feel some anxiety that you are soon to be turned out of your home?’ said Bella.

Rosamond tilted her head on one side while she considered this.

‘I am not sure. It was very good of my grandfather to take me in when my parents died, but he never put himself out for me, you see. It will be very strange to lose all these familiar possessions, to be sure, but it will not overset me, I think.’

‘Well, I wept for days when I had to leave Tommy’s lovely house in Shropshire. So, Rosamond, you must not be surprised if you find yourself suddenly overcome with emotion,’ said Arabella with ready sympathy. ‘Only tell me!’

⋆ ⋆ ⋆

In the event, Rosamond found she had no time for melancholy during the next few days.

She was far too busy completing the inventory, settling the accounts and writing references for all the servants. With the exception of Meggie, whom she retained as her maid, the last of the servants had to be paid off and it was not until she was seated beside Mrs Tomlinson in Lord Ullenwood's elegant travelling carriage three days later that Rosamond allowed herself time for reflection.

'Now, you must not try to be brave,' said Arabella, reaching across to squeeze her hands. 'You may cry as much as you wish, I have several spare handkerchiefs with me.'

'Thank you, but strangely, I do not feel the least bit inclined to cry. Perhaps I am a very cold person.'

'Nonsense,' Arabella was quick to retort. 'You have been very kind to me, and forgive me if I speak bluntly, but I thought the manor a very cold and gloomy house.'

'It is,' Rosamond agreed. 'I had grown so familiar I did not see it until we went through the house, cataloguing each item. And it has grown very shabby, too, because poor Grandpapa could not pay to keep it up. If he had been less proud he might have sold the house, or rented it, and moved into something smaller, where we could have lived much more comfortably. I can see you are not convinced, Bella, but there is nothing comfortable about living in a big house where one cannot afford to have fires in the rooms and tradesmen are always pressing for payment,' She looked down at her fashionable fur-lined pelisse and added ruefully, 'And no money for little luxuries such as new clothes.'

'Oh you poor thing!' cried Arabella. 'You must not mind it, for it is all behind you now. You will find that Elliot lives in the height of luxury and all you need do is enjoy it. Yes yes,' she added hastily as Rosamond opened her mouth to speak. 'I know you will say you must find some occupation and earn your living, but not *immediately*. Dear Rose, you must allow Elliot to take care of you for a few weeks at least. Ah, here we are.'

Rosamond looked out of the window as the carriage slowed and turned off Piccadilly into a quiet side street, at the end of which stood a large town house set back in its own grounds. An icy rain had begun to fall and, as the carriage came to a stand, two footmen hurried forward, each with a large umbrella with which to shelter the ladies as they stepped out of the carriage and walked the few steps to the door. In the hall, flames leapt from the fireplaces set at each end, and Rosamond was at once aware of the warm air on her cheek. As if this was not sufficiently cheering, she was greeted by the kindly smile of the housekeeper, who came forward to help her remove her pelisse, introducing herself as Mrs Trimble. She immediately began apologizing that the marquis was not present to receive his guest.

'He hoped you would forgive him, miss, for he has business to attend to, and says he will join you in the drawing-room before dinner this evening. In the meantime, I am to show you to your rooms, and if there is anything you are wanting for your comfort, I'd be pleased if you would tell me.'

'And does that apply to me, too, Trimble?' asked Arabella, coming up to them.

'Away with you, Miss Bella; you know you only have to ask for anything in this house,' declared the housekeeper with the mock severity of an old and trusted retainer.

'Then perhaps you would warm a little soup for when we have unpacked. We have been up since dawn, and only had time to swallow a mouthful of bread and butter before those awful bailiffs forced us out of the house.'

'Oh you poor dears!' Mrs Trimble threw up her hands in horror. 'Let me take you upstairs without any more delay. Now, Miss Beaumarsh, did you bring your maid?'

'She is following in the baggage coach, with my own woman,' said Arabella, leading the way up the stairs. 'Although I have to say she is not exactly a *lady's* maid.'

'Meggie is a good girl, and very willing,' said Rosamond, biting back a smile.

'I could say as much of a large puppy!' retorted the widow.

'I know,' confessed Rosamond, 'but I could not leave her behind. She has been at Northby since she was a child. I am sure she will learn very quickly.'

'She has been acting as your maid since I arrived and I have yet to discover that she has learned how to hook up a gown! I think — '

'Now hush, Miss Bella,' said Mrs Trimble, bustling in between them. 'Never you mind what anyone says, Miss Beaumarsh, you must make up your own mind,' she said pacifically. 'We shall see how this Meggie of yours goes on, and if she is not suitable we will find her something here. Now, you are to have your usual room, Miss Bella, and I will show Miss Beaumarsh to her apartment.'

Before disappearing into her room, Arabella promised to come and find Rosamond in half an hour and take her downstairs to the breakfast parlour.

'For by then I am sure dear Trimble will have our soup ready!'

* * *

Rosamond was very grateful for her friend's companionship. She did not think she would lose her way in the house, for it was much smaller than Northby Manor, but while Rosamond had felt at home in the vast empty corridors, here there seemed to be an army of servants at every turn. She was not to know that the household was agog with curiosity so see Lord Ullenwood's new charge, convinced he intended to marry her. No one knew how it had started, but as soon as it became known that she was coming to live at Ullenwood House, the rumour spread rapidly through the servants' rooms.

'You take my word for it, Mrs T,' said Cook, in a moment of rare shared confidences over a glass of the master's best Madeira wine, 'a man don't put himself out like that for a chit if he ain't enamoured.'

In consequence, when Rosamond arrived at Ullenwood House, every member of the household was eager for a glimpse of her. The boot boy and scullery maid might be forced to peek out through a basement window, but everyone else found an excuse to make their way through the main rooms and take a look at the woman who had captured their master's heart. Most were disappointed and thought her too small and mouse-like to be of consequence. Why, she couldn't hold a candle to the lively Mrs Tomlinson, but when the housekeeper was applied to for her opinion she would only shake her head and warn them all not to be too hasty.

'She may be quiet,' she said, 'but she is no mouse, you mark my words. The lady is used to running her own household and knows her own mind.'

'They say her grandfather shot hisself and left her penniless,' said the under-footman. 'Gambling, they say. A sinful end.'

'Well, he left her to the master's care, and that shows some good sense,' observed Cook, up to her elbows in flour as she kneaded a large ball of dough. 'But will she make him a good wife, Mrs T? There'll be some changes here if he weds her.'

The housekeeper rose and shook out her skirts, preparing to return to her own room.

'Well, no one's said anything about marriage that I know of,' she declared, 'so I say again let's not be hasty. We shall have to wait and see which way the wind blows. And then there's those precious aunts of the master's. We don't know yet if they approve.'

8

Rosamond dressed with care for her first dinner at Ullenwood House. Taking Arabella's advice she chose a dove-grey gown with a Norwich shawl of plain white to cover her shoulders. Such attire would have been too flimsy for the draughty rooms of Northby Manor, but Lord Ullenwood's town house was compact and warm, with close-fitting windows and heavy curtains to shut out the icy night air, and fires burning in almost every room providing the ultimate luxury.

She accompanied Arabella to the drawing-room, where they found Lord Ullenwood awaiting them. Rosamond felt a little shy at first; all her previous encounters with the marquis had taken place at Northby Manor — familiar ground for her. Now she was a guest in his house and it made her nervous. However, Lord Ullenwood greeted her with friendly civility and soon put her at her ease.

'You have everything you need, Miss Beaumarsh?' He led her to a chair.

'Thank you, yes. Mrs Trimble has been most attentive.'

'And your room is to your liking.'

She smiled up at him. 'Very much. It is very comfortable, and well appointed.'

'You have had the guest rooms decorated since I was last here, have you not, Elliot?' put in Arabella, taking a chair close to Rosamond.

'Yes, and the new wing is finished now.'

She nodded. 'Mrs Trimble showed me. The new ballroom is delightful. You must hold a ball very soon, Cousin.'

'You forget, Bella, your mama has expressly forbidden you to go into Society, which must mean that she would not approve of any such festivities. And even if that were not the case,' he added, as she was about to protest, 'Miss Beaumarsh's situation must preclude anything of that nature.'

'Of course, I had forgotten. But these things should be well planned, Elliot. Should we not start organizing your next ball now?'

His lips twitched.

'No need for that, Bella. When the time comes I need only ask Henry to see to it.'

'Ah.' Mrs Tomlinson pouted. 'The estimable Henry. How is your secretary?'

'Mellor is in good health and currently in Lincolnshire, with my agent.' The marquis turned to Rosamond. 'I want to improve the drainage on my estates there, and they have gone to look at the new plans. If Henry is satisfied, he will bring them back here for me to approve.'

'You place great faith in your secretary, my lord,' remarked Rosamond.

'I do.'

'Yet I suppose that you would normally visit the area yourself,' she added shrewdly. 'I am sorry if I am the cause of upsetting your plans, sir, however unwittingly.'

Arabella cried out at this, but the marquis hushed her.

'Miss Beaumarsh is right. I do usually attend to such things myself, but Henry is more than able to attend to the affair.' A smile gleamed in his eyes. 'He is equally capable of dealing with matters here, but it was my choice that I should be here to look after you.'

Rosamond found herself smiling back at him.

'Then I am very grateful to you, my lord.'

* * *

Dinner was taken in the breakfast-room, Lord Ullenwood explaining that he preferred its informal setting for family dinners.

'Lord yes,' agreed Mrs Tomlinson as she took her seat. 'A snug little dinner will be just the thing to set Rosamond at her ease.'

Rosamond said nothing, but the array of dishes that covered the table was extensive. Her experience of running Northby Manor informed her that Lord Ullenwood's cook had gone to great lengths to display his or her culinary skills. A glazed turkey, boiled neck of mutton, soup, plum pudding and venison pastry were amongst the dishes displayed for the first course, followed by an assortment that included partridges, sweetbreads and apple tart. With the serious business of eating to be undertaken and the servants in attendance, conversation was confined to unexceptional topics, but once the covers were removed, and the gleaming mahogany table was furnished with only their wine glasses and a selection of fine porcelain confit dishes, Mrs Tomlinson began a direct attack upon her cousin.

'So, Elliot, what are your plans for Miss Beaumarsh?'

The marquis dismissed the remaining servants with a languid wave of one hand before replying.

'Why, I have none, at present. I imagine Miss Beaumarsh will want a little time to recover from the tragic events of the past few weeks. Ullenwood House is at her disposal.'

'You are too good, my lord,' murmured Rosamond. 'I am indeed grateful for your assistance, but I hope I shall not need to impose upon you for too long.'

'I find your determination to seek employment very puzzling,' declared Arabella.

Rosamond shook her head.

'I know you find it hard to understand, Bella, but I do not wish to be dependent upon anyone.'

'Except an employer,' put in Lord Ullenwood.

'That, my lord, would be different. I would expect a fair wage for my labour.' She sipped her wine. 'Perhaps Mr Mellor could advise me.'

The marquis shrugged. 'I am not sure he has much experience in the employment of governesses.'

'I was thinking of something more clerical, sir, as I have already told you.'

'You see yourself as an amanuensis, perhaps, or a private secretary? Ask Henry, by all means, but I doubt if he can help you,' he returned, indifferently.

'Perhaps you know someone who would employ Rosamond,' suggested Arabella. 'Could you not recommend her?'

His lip curled. 'My dear Bella, I do not think my recommendation would have quite the effect Miss Beaumarsh desires.'

His cousin gave a sigh of exasperation.

'Heavens, Elliot, you are not at all obliging tonight! Do you not care what becomes of Rosamond? You are the greatest beast in nature if that is so!'

'Your descent into melodrama is unnecessary, Bella,' he replied coldly. 'Miss Beaumarsh is at liberty to make up her own mind what she wishes to do with her life. She knows that it is not necessary for her to seek employment. I have already explained that there are alternatives.'

Rosamond was aware that Arabella wanted to continue the argument, but one look at Lord Ullenwood's implacable countenance made her break in.

'Indeed, I am well aware that Lord Ullenwood has no intention of leaving me a pauper, and that is a great comfort. Perhaps, Bella, we should retire now and leave our host to enjoy his brandy?'

She led the widow away to the drawing-room, where the marquis joined them soon afterwards. When Mrs Tomlinson left the room and they were alone briefly, Rosamund took the opportunity to say, 'I hope you will forgive Arabella her outburst. I think you have not explained to her fully the alternatives you outlined to me.'

'You mean I did not tell her I had offered for you?' he said bluntly. 'Certainly not. Bella would think it the perfect solution and would nag you mercilessly.'

She looked down at her hands, clasped lightly in her lap.

'I thought you had said nothing because you were regretting your rash proposal.'

'No. The proposal stands, madam.' His tone was indifferent. 'The arrangement would be convenient to us both.'

Rosamond suppressed a shiver.

'Convenient it may be, sir, but I should still like to consider other avenues.'

'As you wish.'

⋆ ⋆ ⋆

Over the next few weeks Rosamond did her best to decide upon her future, but she had to admit that the alternatives to Lord Ullenwood's proposal were not attractive. Mr Mellor, the marquis's secretary, returned from Lincolnshire and Rosamond screwed up her courage to approach him. Not that he was in any way unapproachable, for he had an open, friendly countenance, engaging manners and a ready smile. However, when she outlined to him her suggestion that she should find work with some great man of business or politics, his response was similar to that of the marquis, if more tactfully expressed.

'I would not disagree, Miss Beaumarsh, that your education and your experience in running your grandfather's estate qualify you to be of great assistance to some important family; indeed you are in all likelihood better qualified than many an estate manager, but in the instances I know of where women have fulfilled such roles, they have been married to the gentleman, or a member of his family.' Mr Mellor looked faintly apologetic. 'Your presence in a bachelor's household would be viewed askance, and if the gentlemen were to be married, well, do you expect a wife to take kindly to her husband spending the better part of each day alone with a young woman? You might consider becoming a housekeeper, but if that is the case, then you have no need to apply elsewhere: my lord has several houses where there is no one currently installed and I am sure he would allow you to take up residence in any one of them.'

'Yes, thank you, Mr Mellor.'

After this depressing conversation, Rosamond approached the register offices and discovered that a lady in deep mourning was not in an advantageous position. All the available vacancies were to be taken up immediately, and however impatient of convention she might be, it was impossible for her to take employment until she had completed at least a short period of mourning.

★ ★ ★

Her thoughts were given another turn by the arrival of Lady Padiham. Rosamond watched her arrival from an upper landing, and marvelled at the number of trunks and boxes that were carried into the hall. Then she turned her attention to the lady herself, who had removed her pelisse to display a gown that declared to the observant that she was a lady of decided wealth and fashion. She was not a tall woman, and the voluminous folds of her embroidered muslin gown accentuated her ample figure. A white ruff frilled about her short neck above a dark-blue fichu that crossed her large bosom, while a matching turban covered all her hair except a few improbably red curls. Even from her distant viewpoint Rosamond thought she looked to be very good-natured. She saw the marquis come forward to welcome her with a chaste salute upon one scented cheek and heard the lady give a fat chuckle.

'Well, Elliot, I am here, and I hope you are suitably grateful for the effort I have made.'

'I am forever in your debt for this, ma'am.'

'Yes, yes, that is all very well, but take me out of this draughty hall, if you please, and introduce me to this little gel you have taken in.'

Lady Padiham was escorted to the morning-room by her host, and Arabella and Rosamond were summoned to attend her. Lady Padiham greeted them warmly and immediately informed her nephew that while she was perfectly happy to act as his hostess, nothing would persuade her to venture out of doors.

'My dear ma'am, that will not be necessary upon my account,' said Rosamond quickly.

'Miss Beaumarsh lost her grandfather only a month since,' explained the marquis. 'There will be no need for you to take her about for the present time, for she will not be making morning visits or attending balls.' He cast a glance at Mrs Tomlinson. 'Bella will be happy to accompany Miss Beaumarsh upon any necessary outings, but you must see, ma'am, that your presence in my house will prevent the rise of any unpleasant gossip.'

'Yes, of course.' My lady waved one fat, be-ringed hand at him. 'If you were married, Elliot, my presence would not be necessary, but you continue your bachelor life, littering the Town with broken hearts — '

'My dear aunt — ' he expostulated, but she cut him short.

'Do not deny it, Elliot. Even in Herefordshire I hear the news; there is not a month goes by but there is some other female whose hopes you have dashed.'

'But you will not hear that I was the one to raise those hopes in the first place.'

Lady Padiham, a fair-minded woman, had to agree, but she was not to be silenced.

'Can you blame my sisters for trying to find you a bride since you will not take the trouble for yourself?' she continued. 'You prefer to involve yourself with a succession of mistresses — and you need not frown at me so dreadfully, sir. You know I am too lazy to mince my words. Arabella is well aware of your behaviour, and unless Miss Beaumarsh has been a complete recluse I have no doubt she has heard of your reputation. Is that not so, my dear?'

'Yes, ma'am,' murmured Rosamond.

She had been living at Ullenwood House for only a short time, but already on several occasions she had noticed the marquis pick out a scented note from the daily collection of letters and invitations brought to the breakfast table for his attention. Now she bit back a smile as she watched my lord's harsh features darken into a scowl. He reminded her very much of a schoolboy caught out in wrong-doing. At that moment he looked up and caught her eye. For an instant Rosamond feared that her amusement had angered him, but instead his scowl faded and a wry smile curved his lips.

'I shall endeavour to mend my ways while you are in residence, Aunt.'

'Aye, do,' replied Lady Padiham. 'Now, let us be serious. What plans have you for my entertainment, Elliot?'

'Why none, ma'am. I anticipated you would want to live quietly, as you do in Herefordshire.'

'My dear nephew, because I have told you I do not wish to go out does not mean visitors cannot come to see *me*. Of course, there must not be music or dancing; Miss Beaumarsh's bereavement precludes that, but a few guests for supper will do no harm. Indeed it would do the poor child a deal of good, for there is nothing more injurious to the spirits than to be moping about feeling sorry for oneself. Now, there are any number of people I must see while I am in Town, so I suggest a little supper party, Elliot.'

Mrs Tomlinson clapped her hands.

'Oh a splendid idea, Aunt Padiham. When shall it be? Shall I know any of your guests?'

'Next week I think.' She chuckled, and the ruff supporting her chins trembled. 'If Bessborough had not taken Harriet off to

Paris I would have asked her to come, for she is such a dear, sweet woman, but as to the rest, I doubt there will be anyone to interest you, Bella, and no young men for you to captivate, you naughty puss.'

'No, I thought not,' Arabella sighed. 'My uncle was a friend of Addington's, was he not? So I suppose the talk will all be of politics.'

'It will not do you any harm to think of something other than the latest gowns, Bella,' growled Lord Ullenwood.

Arabella pouted, but Rosamond said shyly, 'Was your husband involved in the government, Lady Padiham?'

'Bless you, my love, he died before Pitt fell, but he was a great supporter of Fox, you know. I have kept in touch with all my old friends and I shall invite them to come and see me, if Ullenwood will arrange it. I am sure I do not have the energy to do so.'

'I shall ask Henry to see to it, ma'am,' smiled the marquis. 'All you need do is to be present on the night.'

* * *

'Well, what do you think of my aunt?' asked Mrs Tomlinson as she accompanied Rosamond back to her room later that night. 'She is a little eccentric, and extremely idle, but she is very good-natured.'

Rosamond nodded.

'I like her: she is very droll, and she was very kind to me. Do you think she will invite lots of members of the cabinet to her party? Will they come?'

'Oh, I expect they will, for she is extremely well connected, and although Elliot is not active in politics they will not readily turn down an opportunity to come to Ullenwood House.' Arabella sighed. 'It will be very dull for us, however. Aunt Padiham's friends are all so old! There will be no one to flirt with.'

Rosamond considered the forthcoming supper in a much more hopeful light. She had no desire to flirt with anyone, but if Lady Padiham's guests included men who were active in politics, then it might prove to be just the opportunity she needed to find an employer.

⋆ ⋆ ⋆

With Lady Padiham established at Ullenwood House, life settled into a slow, indolent pattern that Rosamond found irksome in the extreme. If she went out she was heavily veiled and accompanied by Mrs Tomlinson, who was under strict instruction from her cousin to do nothing that would excite public interest or condemnation. Indoors, the two young ladies spent their days sewing, reading, playing the pianoforte or working on their watercolours. Mrs Trimble was a very efficient housekeeper and there was no useful role for Rosamond in the organization of Ullenwood House. The marquis himself was absent most days, joining the ladies for dinner some evenings, but generally keeping clear of what he described acidly to Sir James as a houseful of females.

Lady Padiham never left her room before noon, and whiled away her afternoons entertaining her friends before retiring again to rest before dinner. She explained to Rosamond that she never ventured out of doors during the colder months, but that as soon as the warmer weather arrived she would bestir herself and take a gentle airing in the park. Mrs Tomlinson avoided her aunt's afternoon visitors whenever possible, preferring to exchange notes with her friends on the latest salacious gossip. Rosamond hoped that by being present to help Lady Padiham entertain her guests she might enjoy a little stimulating conversation, and discover someone in need of a clerk.

* * *

It did not take Rosamond long to realize that Lady Padiham had lived retired for a great many years and the friends who remained in Town were more interested in their ailments than in the tenuous peace with France. She was surprised, therefore to find a very fashionable gentleman waiting in the hall one chilly afternoon. For once there were no servants in the hall and he had removed his heavy Benjamin to reveal a well-fitting coat of fine blue wool worn over a garish waistcoat and tight, pale pantaloons that disappeared into a pair of shining Hessian boots.

'Oh,' she stopped. 'Are you waiting to see Lady Padiham? I believe she is entertaining in the morning-room, I am on my way there now . . . '

The man tossed his coat over a nearby chair, swept his curly-brimmed beaver hat from his gleaming fair hair and made her an elegant bow.

'Thank you, ma'am, but no. In fact I did not know she was in Town. I am waiting to see Lord Ullenwood.' He straightened and smiled at her. 'I am sorry, we have not been introduced.'

Rosamond felt her colour rising. How was she to describe herself? The gentleman spared her the trouble.

'You must be Elliot's new ward, Miss

Beaumarsh; do I have that right? How do you do, ma'am? Sir James Ashby, at your service.'

She inclined her head.

'Sir James. Does Lord Ullenwood know you are here? Would you like me to find him?'

'No need, Miss Beaumarsh. Johnson is taking my card up. No, pray, do not run away,' he added quickly as she prepared to leave. 'Tell me how you go on. Is that why Lady P is here, to look after you?'

'I do very well, sir, I thank you. And yes, my lady is a kind and considerate hostess.'

'I believe she is very good-natured, although I would hazard a guess that her acquaintances are a little long in the tooth for you, eh? Dashed if I am not offended that you should think me one of their number!' Rosamond looked up at him quickly, and was reassured by the twinkle in his blue eyes. He continued, 'But how does such a confirmed old bachelor as Elliot cope, having his aunt rule the roost?'

He was smiling, but Rosamond was unsure how to respond to his jest and she was relieved to see the marquis appear at the top of the stairs.

'I cannot answer that, Sir James,' she said, smiling back at him. 'You had best ask Lord Ullenwood himself.'

'Ask me what?' demanded the marquis, coming downstairs.

'How you like having your aunt installed here,' grinned Sir James, coming forward to meet him. 'Elliot, how are you?'

'Well, James, thank you, and I am delighted to have Lady Padiham staying here.'

Sir James gave Rosamond a mischievous look.

'He is always the gentleman, you see, Miss Beaumarsh. I admire that.'

Lord Ullenwood inclined his head.

'You have met my ward, I see.'

'Yes, we introduced ourselves. I hope you do not object?'

'If Miss Beaumarsh does not.'

'Not at all,' she replied, twinkling up at the guest. 'I am only sorry I should have mistaken you for one of my lady's *long in the tooth* acquaintances.'

'Perhaps, James, you would like to come up to my study,' broke in Lord Ullenwood before Sir James could reply. 'If Miss Beaumarsh will excuse us?'

'Of course, my lord.'

Sir James reached out for her hand.

'I am pleased to have met you, Miss Beaumarsh. I know you are in mourning, but I hope — that is, are you receiving visitors yet?'

'No, James, she is not.' Lord Ullenwood's harsh voice cut across the hall.

His guest did not look noticeably dashed, and Rosamond raised her head to give the marquis a challenging look.

'My lord is mistaken,' she said, with great deliberation. 'Naturally I do not go out yet, but Lady Padiham is at home to visitors most days, and I join her to receive them.'

Sir James raised her fingers to his lips.

'Then I shall, of course, look forward to renewing my acquaintance with Lady P.'

'If you have business to discuss with me, Ashby, you had best come up now,' barked the marquis, scowling.

'Lead on, Elliot, I am with you now,' said his friend cheerfully. 'Your servant, Miss Beaumarsh.' He gave her a last, conspiratorial wink before turning to follow his host. 'No need to look as black as thunder, Elliot, I will not keep you long.'

'If it is the usual question, then I can save you the trouble and give you my answer now.' The marquis threw the words over his shoulder as he led the way up to the first floor. 'It is no!'

* * *

Rosamond watched the two men disappear from sight and continued on her way to the morning-room. An encounter with a personable gentleman had lifted her spirits and she very much hoped he would call upon Lady Padiham very soon.

9

The following day Lord Ullenwood invited Rosamond to drive out with him. He had sought her out in the library, towering over her in his drab driving coat with its many shoulder capes that added to his already impressively broad shoulders.

'You hesitate, Miss Beaumarsh. Perhaps you are afraid I shall overturn you.'

'No, I know you are considered a notable whip. I am merely surprised that you should ask me. Is Arabella indisposed?'

'I have not asked Bella.'

'Oh.' She regarded his buckskins and gleaming top boots. 'But you are ready to go — I would need to change my dress.'

'I have this minute sent for my carriage, so I can give you twenty minutes — and wear a warm coat, it is turning very cold.'

Rosamond bridled at his autocratic tone. She was tempted to refuse his offer, but the thought of going out was too appealing, so she merely nodded and hurried away to put on her walking dress.

* * *

'Why were you surprised I should invite you to come driving with me?'

They were heading out into the traffic of Piccadilly and Rosamond did not answer immediately, but watched the marquis controlling his high-stepping team of matched bays as they inched their way through a narrow space between a private coach and a farmer's wagon.

'I was surprised because I thought you were avoiding me. Or, if not me,' she temporized, 'I thought perhaps you were finding it an imposition to have your house suddenly invaded by so many ladies.' She was thankful that her heavy veil concealed her blush, and thought that she would not have dared to say such a thing to the marquis if he had been able to see her face. A glance at his impassive countenance told her nothing of his reaction to her words, and she forced herself to carry on, 'I fear that I have disrupted your life much more than you anticipated, my lord. It was never my intention to be such a burden.'

The marquis guided his team into Hyde Park before replying.

'You are correct. I *have* been avoiding the house since my aunt's arrival. I was under the misapprehension that Lady Padiham would look after you and Bella, and I would be free to continue with my life very much as usual. It was only when Ashby called yesterday that I realized I am neglecting you.'

'You are not!' she cried. 'Oh this is dreadful. I never wanted this! I had not thought that my grandfather's actions would put you to so much trouble.' She clasped her hands and moved restlessly in her seat. 'I had thought — hoped — that I could achieve some measure of independence when Grandfather died, but I have become even more of a burden, and to you, a stranger, upon whom I have no right at all to impose!'

Lord Ullenwood brought the horses to a stand and directed his groom to go to their heads. When he was sure they were under control he laid aside the reins.

'Miss Beaumarsh, Rosamond, hush now!' He took her hands. 'Look at me. Damnation.' With a muttered oath he flicked back the veil from her face. 'That's better. Now, young lady, look at me. Do I look like a man at the end of his endurance? No. Ullenwood House has room and to spare for another dozen guests and servants enough to look after them all.' He squeezed her fingers and smiled at her 'You are not a burden.'

She looked up at him with an anxious frown.

'Have we not driven you from your home?'

The smile grew.

'No. The truth is I rarely dine at home when I am alone. Now, instead of berating yourself for being a nuisance, you should be upbraiding *me* for my lack of attention.'

She blinked and her lip trembled.

'I could not do that, when you have been so kind to me.'

'Kind!' He handed her a snowy handkerchief. 'Here, wipe your eyes. I would guess that for the past few years you have been living with a man who considered nothing but his own comforts, and you have come to think of yourself as having no worth at all. And yet you have spirit, I know that. Where is the woman who would only drink champagne the first time I came to see her?'

'I was so angry that you should presume to order my servants.'

'And quite rightly so. It was an unforgivable piece of impertinence. I beg your pardon for it. If you wish to drink champagne every afternoon then I will ask Johnson to have it ready for you.

She was engaged in wiping her eyes but managed a watery chuckle.

'Now you are being absurd, sir.'

'Yes I am,' he agreed.

He took her chin between the finger and thumb of one hand and tilted up her head.

'Give me my handkerchief and let me wipe away the rest of those tears. They do not become you.'

'No doubt your mistress can shed tears and still look beautiful,' she muttered.

'Of course,' he agreed cordially. 'She can cry at will, without her skin becoming at all blotched, or her nose turning an unbecoming shade of red. The difference, however' — he pinched her chin — 'is that it is all for effect, whereas your emotion is from the heart.' He held her eyes for a moment, then with a slight laugh he released her and drew the veil back over her face. 'Now that we understand one another, I think we should continue our drive. I will not keep my horses standing too long in this cold wind. Let 'em go, Kirkham!'

Despite the chill wind the park was busy with carriages and riders, but although the marquis acknowledged a number of acquaintances he did not stop to speak to any of them. However, it reminded Rosamond of her quest for independence.

'You know so many people, my lord,' remarked Rosamond, 'I am sure there must be at least one amongst them who would be grateful for a little help — with letter writing, perhaps.'

'I am sure there are, but none that would welcome a recommendation from *me*.'

His tone was so implacable that she ventured no further word on the matter, but pinned her hopes on the guests invited by Lady Padiham to her party that evening.

* * *

By the time they returned to Ullenwood House, Rosamond was on the best of terms with her host, and surprised to find she had enjoyed herself more than at any time since leaving Northby Manor. A comment as he handed her down made her pause.

'Do you mean you will not be attending your aunt's party this evening?' she asked, putting up her veil as he led her into the house.

'There is no need for me to be there.'

'Oh.' She was immediately aware of a deep disappointment. 'Remembering our earlier conversation, my lord, you said I should upbraid you for your neglect . . . '

He gave a bark of laughter.

'So I did, and now you throw it back in my face. Baggage! Very well. I have an engagement for the first part of the evening, but I will drop in later, you have my word. Will that do?'

'Thank you sir.' She turned and looked up to the landing as she heard a voice. Mrs Tomlinson was looking down at her from the gallery.

'So there you are, Rosamond! I am so glad you are back. Aunt Padiham has changed her mind on what to serve for supper tonight and has asked me to give Cook her new orders. Do come with me, for you know she will be as cross as crabs to have her plans overset at this late stage. Or better still,' she said, brightening, 'Elliot could tell her.'

He put up his hands.

'Oh no, you shall not drag me into this, Bella.'

'Give me a moment to put off my cloak and bonnet and I shall come with you,' said Rosamond. She glanced up at the marquis. 'I hope you will not lose your cook, my lord.'

'Not a chance of it,' he retorted. 'She may huff and puff, but she will not in any way blame *me* for this upset!'

'What a spiritless creature you are, Lord Ullenwood.' Rosamund laughed and began to make her way up the stairs. 'Wait for me, Bella and we will brave the kitchens together.'

'And I shall ask Johnson to have a glass of champagne ready for you when you return,' the marquis called after her.

'What did he mean by that?' asked Arabella, frowning.

Rosamond blushed and shook her head before hurrying off to her bedchamber.

* * *

For Lady Padiham's party, Mrs Tomlinson had purchased a new gown of Italian sarsenet in pale lilac with a matching head-dress, but Rosamond could not be persuaded to order another new gown and she chose to wear her dove grey silk with a bandeau of white lace secured around her dark hair. A string of pearls about her neck was her only ornament and Lady Padiham nodded in approval of her simple attire, declaring it entirely suitable for a young lady in mourning.

'Of course, I shall not make a great fuss of presenting you,' said my lady, shaking out the folds of her own rose-coloured gown. 'Since you and Arabella are still in mourning you shall not be put forward in any way, but you must watch me, my dears, and if I call you over then it will be to present you to one or two of my particular friends.' She smiled and nodded, setting the golden plumes attached to her turban waving gently above her.

'Has my cousin invited any of his friends tonight, Aunt?' asked Arabella.

'No, he has left everything to me, but he has promised to look in a little later.'

'To make sure we are not enjoying ourselves,' muttered Arabella, pouting.

Lady Padiham was too good-natured to take offence and merely chuckled.

'You must behave yourself tonight, Bella, else I will have to answer for it to your dear mama.'

'So we must sit, mumchance, in a corner like schoolgirls not yet out,' grumbled Arabella as the first guests began to arrive. She flounced down beside Rosamond in a shadowy corner of the room, and tapped her fan angrily against her hand.

'But Bella, you must know most of these guests already,' remarked Rosamond.

'I do, of course, and a duller set one could never imagine. Most are older than Mama.' Bella shivered. 'I am surprised they will venture out on such an icy night!'

'There is a roaring fire, Bella, and it will soon grow more comfortable when everyone has arrived,' replied Rosamond, determined to be cheerful. 'Stay here while I fetch you some mulled wine. That will warm you.'

As the guests came in, Rosamond recognized many of them as my lady's afternoon visitors, and those she did not know she turned to Arabella to enlighten her. She was mindful of her conversations with the marquis and considered that if she was looking for employment it could not be with a young man. Lord Ullenwood seemed to think that such men would misunderstand her motives. Neither should she choose a married man, since Mr Mellor had pointed out that a wife might well object. No, she needed to find an elderly, single gentleman who would welcome her help in matters of business. She therefore watched the guests with interest, and when at length she saw her aunt sitting alone she went over to her.

'What a fascinating evening, ma'am. So many guests: I should dearly like to know who they all are.' She glanced around. 'That gentleman over there, for instance, the one in the puce coat and the red whiskers.'

'Ah, that is Lord Tyneham,' said Lady Padiham. 'Excellent man. Retired from government now, of course, but his grasp of foreign policy is second to none. Addington wanted him to be ambassador in Paris, you know, rather than Lord Whitworth, but he turned it down, said he was too old to be gallivanting over the Continent.'

'I see. And that one? The tall, thin gentleman in the grey bag-wig and chocolate-coloured frock-coat?'

'Matthew Harkstead.' Lady Padiham sighed. 'Dear man. Lost his wife several years ago and has since thrown himself into charitable works.'

'How interesting.' Rosamond considered

the gentleman. Perhaps this was her opportunity. She felt a little jolt of surprise when Lady Padiham offered to present him to her, and could only watch, speechless, as my lady waved an imperious hand and Mr Harkstead wandered over.

'Matthew, you must let me present you to my little friend, Miss Beaumarsh. Northby's granddaughter, you know.'

'Ah yes, I heard about that,' He took her hand and bowed over it. 'A very bad business. My condolences, Miss Beaumarsh.' For all her planning, Rosamond could think of nothing to say. Mistaking her silence for heartbreak, Mr Harkstead patted her hand. 'You must feel it dreadfully, to be wrenched from your family home, with no one to look after you.'

'Excuse me, Matthew, but she has my nephew to advise her,' put in Lady Padiham.

'Ah yes, of course, of course.'

With a bow, Mr Harkstead walked away, and soon afterwards Rosamond returned to her corner seat beside Arabella, the beginnings of a plan taking shape in her head.

* * *

Arabella handed her another cup of mulled wine.

'I am so bored,' she complained. 'Aunt Padiham has told them all about me, so that the ladies only want to sympathize and the gentlemen treat me as if I was their grand-daughter. I wish there was someone here to laugh with.'

'Perhaps there is,' murmured Rosamond, looking towards the door. 'Your cousin has this minute come in.'

Arabella was immediately on the alert.

'Oh famous,' she declared, brightening immediately. 'He has Sir James Ashby with him. Do you know Sir James, Rosamond?'

'I have met him; he came to the house the other day.'

'He is very good company.' She gave a little crow of laughter. 'Oh look, Sir James is coming over. Good evening, sir. I am so pleased to see you.'

He bowed over the widow's hand with practised grace.

'Servant, ma'am. Miss Beaumarsh.'

'We are so happy that you are here,' cried Arabella, clinging on to his fingers. 'I do hope you will stay and talk to us all night.'

'Well, I would be delighted to do so, of course, but I fear I must do my duty and seek out my hostess. Then I hope to come back to you.'

'Yes, do hurry back,' begged Arabella. 'You

can have no notion how dull we are finding the company.'

Sir James put up a hand and said with a laugh in his voice, 'Have a care, ma'am, you must know that most of these people are friends of mine!'

Rosamond seized her chance.

'Are most of them in the government, Sir James?'

'Well, some of 'em, certainly.'

'How fascinating. What a pity that we have agreed not to seek introductions this evening, for there are several persons here whom I would dearly like to know more of . . . Lord Tyneham, for instance.'

He smiled at her.

'Would you? Well let me go and do the pretty by Lady P, then, if you wish, I will present some of these fascinating gentlemen to you.'

Scarcely able to believe her good fortune, Rosamond thanked him prettily and watched him walk away. Arabella tutted impatiently beside her.

'Rosamond I am disappointed in you. Sir James is by far the most attractive gentleman here tonight and all you can do is ask him to introduce you to those dreary old men.'

'I did not ask him, he volunteered,' Rosamond corrected her. 'And besides, I hope to persuade one of those dreary old men to employ me!'

* * *

Her optimism was short-lived. True to his word, Sir James came over presently with Lord Tyneham beside him. Arabella persuaded Sir James to take her over to join Lord Ullenwood on the far side of the room and Rosamond was left alone, doing her best to charm her new acquaintance without fear of his being dazzled by the vivacious widow. Lord Tyneham was very courteous, but so deaf that conversation was extremely difficult. At length she learned that he had no interest in public life and now devoted himself to nothing more strenuous than a stroll in the Green Park with his beloved spaniels. Lord Tyneham clearly did not suit her purpose, neither did the other gentlemen whom Sir James obligingly presented to her, either being too old, too infirm, or with no interests at all except for hunting and fishing. She helped herself to another glass of mulled wine and sat down to rethink her strategy. On the far side of the room she saw Arabella laughing and talking with Sir James and the marquis. She scowled as she finished her wine. It was so disobliging of Lord

Ullenwood not to help her to find employment. She was sure he could do so if he wished. Sir James had been very helpful, but since he had no idea why she wanted an introduction to any of these gentlemen he could not be blamed for presenting those he thought most interesting. She took a glass of champagne from the tray of a passing servant and sipped it. She decided to join Arabella, but even as she rose to cross the room she caught sight of Mr Harkstead sitting alone by a window. She would have one last try. As she approached, he stood up and smiled at her in such a fatherly way that she was encouraged. Smiling back, she sank down on to the sofa.

'I do hope you are not finding the company tiresome, Mr Harkstead,' she began.

'Not at all, Miss Beaumarsh.'

'Perhaps you are fatigued,' she continued. 'Such a busy life as you must have. My aunt tells me you are involved in many charitable works, I wonder how you can find time for it all.'

'One is obliged to organize one's time, naturally,' he replied, sitting down beside her. 'But you are right, one rarely has a moment to oneself, for there are committees to attend, working parties, not to mention the petitions. People are forever knocking on my door, begging me to help them. You see, I am even now in the process of setting up a new scheme to alleviate the sufferings of the deserving poor . . . '

'And do you have anyone to help you?' she asked, taking a sip of her champagne.

'I have a clerk, of course . . . '

'And I am sure he is very useful, but he cannot understand the finer points of your charities.'

'No, my dear, you are quite right. How acute of you.'

Rosamond thought of the estimable Henry.

'Would you, for example, trust him to make judgements on your behalf?'

'Oh no, no, that would never do.'

She took another sip for courage.

'I would very much like to help you with your work, Mr Harkstead.'

'You would?' he said, surprised.

'Oh yes, very much so. You see, since my grandfather's death I have spent far too much time doing nothing. I want an interest that I can throw myself into wholeheartedly.'

'Well, that is very . . . admirable, but I do not see — '

'From what you have told me I think I could help you with your work, sir, take some of the burden from your shoulders: it must be very lonely for you, with no one waiting for you at the end of the day to share your worries.'

'That is true,' he said, much struck. 'I carry all these cares with me, day and night. To have someone who could ease that burden would be an advantage.' He paused. 'Your glass is empty, Miss Beaumarsh. Let me find you another . . . '

He signalled to a footman and was soon handing Rosamond another glass of champagne. Her head was beginning to spin a little, but the bubbling wine seemed to help her to express her thoughts, so she took another, larger sip.

'I thought that you were under Lord Ullenwood's protection,' remarked Mr Harkstead.

'Well, I am, of course, but it is not always very comfortable.'

'Ah, I understand,' he said quickly.

Rosamond wondered what he meant by that, but she let it pass and said eagerly, 'I would very much like to be independent.'

'But will Lord Ullenwood not object?'

'Oh no,' she replied airily. 'We have discussed it, and in truth, I think he would be very pleased to be rid of me.' She fixed him with what she hoped was an intelligent look. 'You see, I like to be busy — I want an occupation.'

'Do you now?'

'Yes, sir, for I do so dislike to be idle, and if you were looking for someone, I am sure I could be of use to you.'

He gave her hand a fatherly pat.

'I am sure you could, my dear.'

She took another sip of champagne. This was going very well!

'Of course, the problem would be finding somewhere to live.' She considered again the estimable Henry, who had lodgings in nearby Jermyn Street.

'Well, there is no need to let that worry you,' said Mr Harkstead. 'I could find you a snug little house.'

'That is exceedingly kind of you! But we will need to discuss terms, of course.'

'Terms?'

'Well, yes. You will want to know just what I can do . . . '

Mr Harkstead put up a hand and said hastily, 'I do not think we should discuss that here! Perhaps it would be best if you came to see me tomorrow, my dear. I live but a step away, in Dover Street. Come to me at, say two o'clock, and we will discuss everything more fully.'

Rosamond beamed at him.

'Why, thank you, sir. I shall.'

When Mr Harkstead had gone Rosamond

remained on the sofa and considered her success. She had not needed Lord Ullenwood's help after all, which was a great source of satisfaction. She felt a little light-headed, and put down her glass, thinking that perhaps she should not drink anything more. In fact, she was feeling a little sleepy, and was content just to lean back on the sofa and close her eyes . . .

* * *

'Rosamond, where have you been?'

She opened her eyes to find Arabella standing over her. She reached out and pulled her down beside her.

'You will never guess! I have found someone who will hire me as his secretary.'

'No!'

'Yes! Mr Matthew Harkstead.'

Arabella looked across the room at the thin, ascetic-looking man who was even now taking his leave of Lady Padiham.

'Are you quite sure?'

Rosamond nodded.

'Yes. We discussed it fully. He is extremely busy, and thinks I could be of great use to him. I am to see him tomorrow, to agree terms.'

Mrs Tomlinson drew back.

‘Surely you do not mean to go to see him alone?’

‘But of course. Once I am working for him I shall not be able to have my maid in attendance.’

‘And does Elliot know?’

‘No,’ said Rosamond, ‘And I do not mean to tell him, at least until it is all agreed, so I beg you will say nothing of it, Bella.’

‘Very well, if you insist.’

‘I do. This is very important to me, and since your cousin seems to think I cannot manage these things for myself, I shall take great pleasure in proving him wrong.’

10

At precisely two o'clock the next day Rosamond was on the doorstep of a neat, freshly painted house in Dover Street. The cold had deepened overnight and a slight fall of snow had left icy patches on roads and flagways. Rosamond huddled into her fur-lined pelisse and buried her hands in her muff to protect them from the raw wind that was biting at her nose and cheeks, despite her veil. She knocked resolutely and shifted impatiently from one cold foot to another. At length the door opened and she was shown inside. She was heartened when the servant indicated that she was expected, and led her up the stairs to a spacious drawing-room.

'Oh.' She stopped in the doorway. 'I thought Mr Harkstead would want to see me in his office, or study?'

'I was instructed to show you in here, miss.' The footman's patent indifference was unnerving.

Rosamond found her courage seeping away. She squared her shoulders and moved into the room towards the fireplace.

'Very well,' she responded cheerfully. 'I will

warm myself here by the fire while I wait for Mr Harkstead.'

It was very warm in the room. The fire had obviously been burning all morning, and Rosamond was cheered by this: Mr Harkstead must be a man of easy means to afford such a luxury. In her albeit limited experience, most households only lit fires in a room just before they were used. She heard the door open and turned to see that Mr Harkstead had entered.

'Good day to you, Miss Beaumarsh. I am delighted you could come.'

'We made an appointment sir,' she said briskly. 'It would not be very businesslike of me to let you down.'

'No, no, of course not. Let me help you to take off your coat. I am sure you will feel more comfortable. And perhaps your bonnet? You will feel the benefit more when you go back outside. Dear me, what was Perkins thinking, not to help you with them? That's better. Now my dear, come and sit down beside me here, on the settee.'

Rosamond would have preferred a chair, but the only one near the fire now held her coat and bonnet. She sat on the edge of the settee, suddenly ill at ease. She tried to concentrate.

'When would you want me to begin, sir?'

Mr Harkstead smiled at her.

'I thought we might begin today. No point in wasting time, is there, my dear?'

She ran her tongue over her dry lips.

'No, I suppose not. But there are things to be discussed first.'

He moved a little closer.

'Such as?'

Rosamond shifted away and found herself pressed against the carved mahogany arm of the settee.

'S-salaries, sir. And — and contracts.'

Mr Harkstead waved a hand.

'Oh I do not think we need to worry about contracts. I have never found it necessary in the past.'

'H-have you not?'

'No. My previous ladies have all been very happy with the terms.'

'Oh.' Rosamond was surprised. 'So you have had other ladies working for you, sir.'

'Why, yes, of course. I do not think you will find me ungenerous. Would you like to take off your gloves, my dear?'

She swallowed and tried to sound business-like as she drew off her kid gloves.

'You would like me to take some notes for you, perhaps, or — or draft a letter so that you can see how neatly I write? You will surely need some evidence of my abilities.'

'Yes, yes, we will come to that.'

'Then perhaps you will show me where you would like me to work, sir. Do you have a desk for me, perhaps?'

Mr Harkstead's pale eyes widened a little.

'A desk? Why yes, yes, all in good time. For now we will start in here, I think.' He took the gloves from her and tossed them aside. 'I confess I was a little surprised when you approached me last evening, my dear. I did not realize Ullenwood was quite so liberal about these matters.'

She frowned. 'What matters, sir?'

'To keep you in his house, and under his aunt's nose, too.' He took her hands. 'I commend him for that, but then, you are not quite in the common style, one could be mistaken for thinking you were perfectly respectable.'

She looked down to see that he had pulled her hand on to his thigh. She snatched it away.

'I am perfectly respectable! I think — *oh*!'

Before she could move he had pounced on her, taking her in a surprisingly strong clasp and covering her mouth in a hot, wet kiss. Rosamond struggled, the hard wooden arm of the settee digging into her back as he pushed against her. Panic shuddered through her. She squirmed, sliding off the seat and on to her knees to escape him.

'No, no, sir — this is not what I had in mind!' she gasped.

'It is precisely what I had in mind!'

He reached for her again. With a shriek she tried to get up but he caught her arm and pulled her down on to the floor. She struggled furiously and heard the muslin around her neck tearing. He pinned her to the floor.

'Now, now, my dear,' he gasped, his breath hot on her face. 'You cannot promise me so much and then say me nay.' He began to unbutton the fall flap of his knee breeches.

'Mr Harkstead! I told you I wanted to work for you: as a clerk.'

'Nonsense. I know exactly what you were asking of me. So, let me try the merchandise, my dear, then we will talk terms.'

'No!' She turned her head to avoid his mouth, struggling and kicking. Her foot knocked over a little side table, but she could not dislodge his weight pushing down on her. His hands were reaching for her bodice now, ripping away her muslin fichu. She tried to grab his wrists, almost sobbing with frustration.

'What the devil do you think you are doing?'

Lord Ullenwood's furious voice thundered

around the room. The next moment Hark-stead's crushing weight was lifted from her. With shuddering cry, Rosamund turned on her side and curled up, sobbing. She hardly noticed the sounds of punches and grunts, or the crash of breaking furniture, but then there was silence, and she felt a gentle hand on her shoulder.

'Rose?' The marquis was kneeling beside her, speaking softly. 'Has he hurt you?'

She took several deep breaths, trying to recover her senses.

'N-no, not really. I — '

'How dare you come into my house and assault me!' Mr Harkstead's voice, quivering with anger, cut across her. 'I will have you thrown out. Perkins, Perkins!'

'If you are calling for your man he is lying at the foot of the stairs,' barked the marquis. He turned back to Rosamond. 'Can you stand? Let me help you.'

'Thank you.' She climbed unsteadily to her feet. 'I am better now,' she said, but her fingers clung to his hand.

'You scoundrel!' shrieked Harkstead, advancing a little, but still keeping a chair between him and his assailant. 'I will have the law on to you! I have friends in the government — '

Rosamond winced and shrank against Lord Ullenwood, who put his arms about her.

'I am sure they will be interested to learn how you tried to seduce an innocent lady,' he snarled. 'Now be quiet, Harkstead, or I shall be obliged to knock you senseless.' He removed his arms from around Rosamond and stepped over to pick up her pelisse. 'Come, put this on. I will take you home.'

She did not move. Shock had given way to remorse and Rosamond felt the tears beginning to sting her eyes. The marquis gripped her shoulder and gave her a little shake.

'You must be brave a little longer, Rose.'

Drawing another, shuddering breath she nodded and straightened her torn fichu, then she allowed him to help her into her pelisse. Her hands fumbled with the buttons and he pushed them aside and fastened the pelisse for her. When he had finished she picked up her bonnet and managed to tie a creditable bow.

'That's better.' The marquis smiled encouragingly. 'Here.' He put the string of her muff over her head and held out her kid gloves. 'You will need these, it has started to snow.' He led her to the door, then stopped and turned back to face Harkstead, who was still standing behind a chair, an angry bruise beginning to darken his cheek. 'For the lady's sake I shall take this no further,' he said, his voice cutting like steel. 'But should I find that word of this has leaked out, I will hunt you down and destroy you, Harkstead, do you understand?'

With the marquis standing beside her, Rosamond was able to steal a look at Mr Harkstead. He was glowering at them, but his hunched shoulders and frightened countenance turned her fear to pity. She squeezed Lord Ullenwood's arm.

'Please, let us go.'

The winter's day had reached a grey, overcast twilight and, as they stepped out onto the street the icy air caught in Rosamond's throat and made her gasp. She clung to Lord Ullenwood. He glanced down at her.

'Shall I find a cab?'

'No, I would prefer to walk, I think.'

'Be careful, then. The path may be slippery.'

He led her along the street. It was snowing lightly, tiny flakes that swirled across the icy ground. Rosamund screwed up her courage to speak.

'Why did you come for me?'

'Arabella told me what you were about. She was uneasy that you had gone out without your maid, and came to me for advice.'

Rosamond hung her head.

'I think I have been very foolish,' she said in a small voice.

'Damned foolish,' he said brutally.

She bit her lip.

'No doubt you will say I should have listened to you.'

'No. You are such an innocent I should have made it clearer just what could befall you.'

They had reached Piccadilly and Rosamond hesitated.

'I — I do not want to go back just yet. They — Bella — will be looking out for me, and I am not ready . . . '

'Then let us walk in Green Park,' he suggested. 'It is only a little out of our way, and it will give you time to compose yourself.'

He guided her across the busy thoroughfare and into the park. The icy weather had driven off the crowds and even the hawkers were now hurrying off to find warmth and shelter. Very soon they were alone on the path and the falling snow muted the sounds of the traffic until they seemed to be walking in a silent world of their own. Rosamond knew she had to thank the marquis for coming to her rescue and started haltingly to express her gratitude. He cut her short.

'If you had told me of your plans I could

have warned you against it. Whatever possessed you to go and see that man alone?'

'I — I heard that he is very well respected, and he told me himself how busy he has become with all his charitable works.'

'And I suppose you offered him your . . . services.'

'Yes.'

'Good heavens, girl, surely you must realize what he thought you were offering?'

'I do *now*, of course, but last night, it seemed so simple . . . '

He gave an exasperated sigh.

'Harkstead, of all people. The man would have had to be a saint to resist you. Harkstead may be involved in a dozen good works but he is no saint! Damnation, I almost feel sorry for him.'

'Well, I do not!' she retorted with a flash of her old spirit. 'I m-made it very p-plain to him that he had mistaken my meaning and he — he s-still t-tried to — ' She broke off, hunting in her reticule for her handkerchief.

Lord Ullenwood drew out his own and handed it to her. After giving her a moment to wipe her eyes he said again, 'I still do not understand how you settled upon Harkstead.'

She blew her nose defiantly.

'You think I did not listen to your advice, but I *did*. From what you had said I had already decided that a young man would not suit, and then Mr Mellor pointed out that a married man might find that his wife objected — '

'Undoubtedly.'

She winced, but carried on.

'So, so I thought that an o-older man would be the most suitable.' She drew a deep breath. 'I was wrong and I am very sorry to have put you to so much trouble.'

'You deserve to be whipped for what you have done,' he retorted. 'I told you from the start that this scheme of yours could not work.'

'Yes, you did. I should have paid more heed to you.'

'And it is unnecessary,' he continued as if she had not spoken. 'If you really cannot bring yourself to marry me, then I have already said that I shall make you an allowance.'

She stopped.

'You would still marry me after — after what has occurred?'

'Nothing has occurred. Harkstead will keep quiet about today, believe me.'

'But . . . '

'No, it is obvious to me that you need someone to look after you.' He reached out and lifted her veil, gently dropping it back over the crown of her bonnet. 'Well, Miss Beaumarsh, shall we be married and put an end to all this nonsense?'

She stared up at him, her thoughts in chaos. She did not consider herself romantic, but occasionally she had allowed herself to dream of receiving a proposal of marriage. Never in her wildest imaginings had it been in such a setting, in the fading light of a snowy winter's day with the cold pinching at her toes.

'Are you sure that it is what you wish?' she asked him.

'I have already explained to you that I must marry. I think we should rub along together very well, but if you would prefer it, I will settle an allowance upon you and you may have your independence. I will find you a house and a suitable companion, although at this moment I can think of no one who could prevent you from indulging in these madcap schemes of yours. Put that rational mind of yours to work for a moment and consider how convenient marriage would be for both of us.' He smiled down at her and she forgot about her icy toes. 'You had as well marry me, my dear and be done with it.'

She swallowed. Suddenly she was too tired to fight for her independence any longer. What did it matter that they did not love each other? It was time she put aside such childish dreams and considered her future logically.

'Very well, sir, thank you. I would be happy to be your wife, if you think we should suit.'

'Good. Then let us go back and tell Bella and my aunt the news. They will both be delighted, I am sure.'

They began to retrace their steps. It was snowing harder now and by the time they reached Piccadilly the road was turning white with snow settling on top of the ashes that had been thrown down on the icy cobbles. There was not much traffic, but as they approached the turning to Ullenwood House there was a commotion a little further along the road. Voices were raised, the shrill, frightened neighing of a horse and the noise of scraping metal filled the air.

'There has been an accident,' she said, peering through the gloom. 'Someone is hurt: do let us go and see if we can help.'

As they approached the scene the nature of the commotion was clear. A wagon was resting at a drunken angle on the remains of a shattered wheel. A young boy was standing in front of the two horses, trying to hold them steady and being almost lifted off the ground as they raised their heads and snorted anxiously. A crowd was gathered on the flagway and Rosamond could not see past them, but Lord Ullenwood stepped forward and looked over their heads.

'James! Make way, there, let me through!'

Rosamond followed closely as he pushed his way through the crowd and she saw Sir James Ashby lying on the ground, one leg lying beneath him at an unnatural angle.

'What has happened here?' demanded the marquis.

A heavily built man in a cap and muffler who was kneeling beside Sir James stood up and touched his forelock.

'Drayhorse fell on 'im, gov'nor. One of the wheels collapsed and all mayhem broke out, see. This gentleman stepped forward to help and the mare slipped on the cobbles.' He gave a little shrug. 'It's my dray, you see, guv'nor. Thankfully, though, the 'orse is as right as rain.'

Sir James had been lying with his eyes closed, but now he opened them.

'That you, Elliot? Damme but I am glad to see you. Can you get me out of here? I hate being gawped at like some freak show.'

Rosamond had thrown back her veil and dropped to her knees beside the injured man.

'I think the leg is badly broken,' she said. 'We must get him indoors.'

'We can carry him home,' offered the drayman eagerly.

'My house is closer,' muttered the marquis, kneeling to inspect the injured leg.

'Yes, let us take him there, but quickly, it is too cold for him to be lying here,' said Rosamond urgently. She turned to the drayman. 'We will need something to carry him. Pull out one of those window boards, we can use it as a litter.'

'But we was just about to shut up,' objected the shopkeeper, who was part of the crowd.

'Then your assistant can help to carry Sir James to Ullenwood House,' replied Rosamond. 'That way you will be sure of getting your shutter returned to you. And you, boy.' She gestured to a tow-headed youngster who was staring open-mouthed at the proceedings. 'You look like a bright young man: would you like to earn yourself a shilling? Run and fetch the doctor and bring him to Ullenwood House and you will find a shilling waiting for you — and an extra sixpence if you are especially quick! Can you tell him your doctor's direction, my lord?'

The marquis had been attending to Sir James, but now he nodded and gave the boy the information. As the boy ran off, he turned back to his friend.

'I think your leg is broken, James. We will have to move it very carefully.'

'Aye, do what you must,' gasped Sir James,

his face very white. 'Only hurry up about it.'

Rosamond called to the men to bring the shutter closer.

'Put it down here, beside the gentleman. We will need several of you to lift him — carefully now — and my lord, you had best look after his injured leg.'

It was the work of a few moments to put Sir James on to the shutter, but the pain of the movement rendered him unconscious.

'And I am glad of it,' remarked Rosamond as she and the marquis led the way to Ullenwood House. 'I hope he will remain senseless until we have him safe in a bed.'

'Tell me, Miss Beaumarsh, are you always so managing?'

She gave a little chuckle.

'I did rather take over, did I not? But it was so clear what needed to be done, and I am sure if I had not spoken up you would have done so.'

'Undoubtedly. Although I would not have been so rash as to promise that boy as much as a shilling for fetching the doctor.' His dark eyes glinted down at her. 'Do you *have* a shilling?'

She had the grace to blush and wished she had thought to replace her veil and hide her face from his sharp eyes.

'Well, no. I thought . . . '

He laughed and squeezed her hand as it rested in the crook of his arm.

'I know exactly what you thought, Miss Beaumarsh, and you are quite right. I do not begrudge a shilling for my friend. Or even, should the boy be very quick, one-and-sixpence!'

* * *

They reached the house and the marquis directed the men to carry their burden up to one of the guest rooms. Rosamond accompanied them, but once Sir James was laid on the bed he dismissed her along with the litter-bearers.

'Managing you may be but you are nevertheless a single woman, and I will not allow you to undress Sir James. My man Davis and I will attend to that.'

'I shall look out for the doctor, then, and bring him up,' she said.

* * *

The doctor arrived a short time later and hurried into the hall, where he divested himself of his hat and cloak in a scattering of frosty snowflakes. He was a sensible-looking man, who appeared unruffled by the garbled and highly coloured account he had received of carnage on the high street. Rosamund paid off his little escort, and watched the ragged urchin run off into the snow, hoping he would not have his largesse wrested from him by his older and larger companions.

'I understand there is only one casualty, ma'am?'

Rosamond turned to the doctor and found herself being regarded with a fatherly eye.

'Yes, sir. Sir James Ashby — you might know him, since he is a friend of Lord Ullenwood. I understand a horse slipped on the ice and fell upon his leg. I will take you up to see him. The horse was unhurt,' she added, then wondered if this sounded too frivolous.

The guest room showed little signs of its early confusion. Sir James was dressed in what she suspected was one of Lord Ullenwood's nightshirts and lying between crisp white sheets. A fire had been kindled and was blazing merrily, the curtains had been pulled across the window and candles burned around the room. They found only the marquis in attendance and as they entered, Rosamond saw the look of relief upon his face.

'In good time, sir. I have given Ashby a little laudanum but he has fainted off again.'

The doctor put down his bag.

'Then we will waste no time in getting the examination over and done with while he feels no pain. Perhaps, ma'am, you would so good as to find me some bandages.'

* * *

The next few hours proved to be an anxious time. The doctor confirmed that the leg was indeed badly broken, but by the time he was ready to set it, Sir James was semi-conscious again. Rosamund had wanted to remain and help, but the pain of the injury made the patient cry out, and begin to curse his tormentors so eloquently that the marquis insisted she leave the room. Rosamond went to her room to change her gown then, unable to settle, she went in search of Mrs Tomlinson. She found her in the drawing-room, frowning over her tambour frame.

'Rosamond! Thank heaven. How is Sir James? Mrs Trimble told me what had happened but Elliot had given instructions that I was not to be allowed near the sick-room.' She was very indignant, but ruined the effect by adding thoughtfully, 'Which is a very good thing, really, because I am dreadfully sensitive, and faint off at the merest thought of blood or pain.'

'Then I am very glad you did not come in,' replied Rosamond, 'because there was plenty of both. Poor Sir James's leg is in a very bad way. Doctor Miles is even now trying to set it.'

'And have they sent you away because it is so horrible?'

Rosamond's grey eyes twinkled.

'No, I was banished because Sir James's language is not fit for a lady's ears.'

Arabella clapped her hands to her mouth and gave a little crow of laughter.

'Oh poor man! He is always so much the gentleman that he must indeed be suffering. Oh well, there is nothing we can do for him at the moment so we will have to wait for Elliot to come downstairs. I have told Cook to hold dinner, and Aunt Padiham is going to dine in her room, because late meals do not agree with her constitution. Which suits me very well,' Bella continued, patting the sofa beside her, 'because I want you to tell me everything.'

'There is not much to tell,' said Rosamond, sitting down. 'We saw the wagon in Piccadilly with a broken wheel — '

Arabella stopped her.

'Not about *that* — what happened when you went to see Mr Harkstead?'

'Oh, Mr Harkstead.'

'Yes. I am sorry I sent Elliot after you, but I was very worried about you.'

'It is no matter,' said Rosamond, hoping her face would not betray her. 'Mr Harkstead did not suit me and — and Lord Ullenwood arrived in time to bring me home.'

'Oh, is that all?' cried Arabella, disappointed.

'Yes,' affirmed Rosamond. 'Perhaps I should go to Lady Padiham, she may be anxious to know how Sir James goes on.'

'No, I told you, she is dining in her room and she does not like to be disturbed when she is eating. You shall not go away until I know everything! What did Mr Harkstead say, why did he not suit? Last evening you were so excited about the prospect of working for him.'

Rosamond realized that her friend would not let the matter rest. She would worry at it like a dog with a bone until she knew everything — unless there was an even tastier morsel Rosamond could give her. In desperation she said, 'It does not matter at all now, because I — I have agreed to marry your cousin.'

11

Arabella's silence was everything that Rosamond could have hoped for. It lasted for a full minute, then she gave a beaming smile and swept Rosamond into a fierce embrace.

'Oh, Rose, that is wonderful. You and Elliot! I had not dreamed — I had no notion of this. Elliot! But when was this arranged?' She took Rosamond's hands and said eagerly, 'Was there perhaps a long-standing engagement between you — did your grandfather object to the match?'

'No, no, nothing like that.'

'No, of course not, for if that had been the case he would not have left you to Elliot's care.'

Rosamond began to wonder if she had been wise to speak: she was not sure how much the marquis would want her to divulge of their convenient arrangement. She was thankful to see Lord Ullenwood come in at that moment. Arabella immediately flew across the room to him.

'Elliot, you sly thing. Rose has just told me the news. How is it that you have said nothing to me?'

Rosamond sent the marquis a beseeching look. His glance flickered over her, but as his impassive countenance did not change she could not be sure he had understood her.

'Well?' demanded Arabella, clutching his arm and walking with him towards the fire.

'With Lord Northby's demise so recent we decided not to make an announcement.'

Arabella almost stamped her foot in exasperation.

'Oh I know that, but when was it agreed between you? I thought Rose was determined to remain single.'

'I — I wanted a little time to make up my mind,' stammered Rosamond.

'Well, of course,' said the widow, 'I always thought your determination to take paid employment was nonsensical but you were so set on it. Even last night you said — '

'Bella, I thought you at least would acknowledge that a lady may change her mind,' remarked my lord, looking amused.

'Yes, of course,' she said. 'Oh, I am so pleased for you both.' She clapped her hands and gave a little laugh. 'And what Mama and the other aunts will say — '

'You will tell no one, Bella, if you please,' ordered the marquis.

'No, of course not, if you insist.'

'I do.'

'But they must know sometime,' she argued. 'And as soon as they have word of it they will all descend upon you, determined to inspect your future bride.'

'I know, and I have no intention of subjecting Miss Beaumarsh to that.'

'So what will you do?'

'We shall be married by special licence within the week and go abroad immediately after the ceremony.'

'Pray stop teasing your cousin, my lord,' laughed Rosamond, but as her eyes met his, the laughter died away.

'Y-you are serious?'

'I am,' he said gently. 'But I think we should discuss it in private, first, do not you?'

'My dear Rose, you are as pale as your lace,' declared Mrs Tomlinson. She added, with rare sensitivity, 'I think perhaps I should leave you to talk. Elliot, you are not to bully her! Dinner is another hour yet, so I shall come back then.'

Rosamond watched her fly out of the room, leaving behind her a stillness and silence that was unnerving.

'I think my cousin has rarely shown more tact,' observed Lord Ullenwood.

'Yes.' Rosamond swallowed. 'How is Sir James?'

'He is sleeping. The doctor gave him a draught to make him more comfortable. His leg is broken in two places. The doctor has set it, but James cannot be moved, at least for the next few weeks.'

She gave a sigh of relief.

'Then there can be no question of your leaving Town, sir.'

'On the contrary.' He walked to the fireplace and rested one arm on the mantelshelf, gazing down into the fire. The flames illuminated his face, highlighting the smooth, strong planes of his cheek. Rosamond waited patiently and at last he continued. 'You may recall James saying that he was due to go to France at the end of the week. He was to deliver a message to Lord Whitworth, the ambassador in Paris.'

'Surely the message can be sent by courier? We are at peace with France now.'

'A very uneasy peace. It is likely that any letters sent to France will be intercepted. James has been entrusted with a message to be delivered direct to the ambassador: he is instructed to give it only into Whitworth's hands. It is very important and highly secret.' He looked at her. 'After the doctor had left us, James explained it all to me. He wants me to go in his stead.'

'I see.' She bit her lip, considering the matter. 'I do not see that you need to be married to go to France, sir.'

'True. I have business in Paris that could account for my visit, and that was my initial intention, to go alone. However, now Arabella knows we are to be married, I wager the secret will be out within a se'ennight.'

'Is — is that so very bad?'

'My aunts would descend upon the house, intent upon knowing all about you and the circumstances of our arrangement, and I should not be here to support you.'

'Are they so terrible then?' she asked, smiling a little.

'Dragons,' he replied cheerfully. He moved away from the fireplace and sat down beside her. 'They want only the best for the house of Ullenwood, and while I am sure they will approve of you, I would not want to subject you to the ordeal of meeting them without me beside you. That is why I suggest that we marry immediately and fly to France.'

'But that would look as if you were afraid of them,' she objected.

He grinned.

'Everyone knows that is the case.'

She looked down at her hands, clasped lightly in her lap.

'And perhaps that you are ashamed of your bride.'

He reached out and took her fingers in his own.

'That is not so, and could never be. When you are out of mourning I shall introduce my new marchioness to Society with all the pomp and ceremony I can muster.' She blushed. He took her chin in one hand and tilted it up until she found herself looking into his eyes. 'Well, will you come with me?'

'Yes, my lord. Not because I am afraid of facing your aunts, but because if you go alone I shall be afraid for you. Since my grandfather's death you are the only friend I have in the world.'

The gleam of teasing amusement left his face, and he regarded her with a solemn, unreadable look.

'That is very humbling,' he said at last. 'I pray I shall not let you down.'

* * *

'So, is it all decided?'

Mrs Tomlinson looked from Rosamond to the marquis. They were at last alone in the dining-room. The covers had been removed and Johnson had ushered the footmen out of the room in his usual unhurried style. Lord Ullenwood looked around to make sure the door was firmly closed.

'Yes, Cousin. We are to be married and off to France for a honeymoon.'

'There will be no time for Rosamond to buy her bride clothes.'

'I shall be able to buy gowns in Paris,' said Rosamond.

Arabella's eyes lit up.

'Heavens, yes! Oh, you must bring back a really dashy dress for me. I wish I was coming with you.'

'I need you here, Arabella,' put in Lord Ullenwood. 'To look after Aunt Padiham. And Sir James.'

'Oh goodness, I had forgotten all about the poor man!' cried Arabella in mock dismay. 'How can you think of leaving the country when your friend is laid up in your house?'

'Very easily, if there is the possibility of my aunts descending upon me. James is too sick to require my company for a few weeks. I have sent for his valet to come and attend him, and the doctor will call regularly.'

'Well, then, what am I to do?'

'You, sweet cousin, will have the run of my house while I am away. I rely upon you to keep Aunt Padiham entertained. I shall leave her in charge here but I doubt she will bestir herself. Ask Henry for any monies you may need.'

'So I may talk to Cook about the menu.'

'Yes.'

'And order flowers for the main rooms?'

'If you think it necessary, although you will not be entertaining, and there will be very few blooms at this time of the year.'

'I am sure Aunt Padiham will appreciate the effort, my lord,' put in Rosamond sweetly, 'Despite the expense.'

My lord cast a scorching glance at his betrothed, but she returned his look with a bland smile.

'Yes, and I must have something to do,' agreed Arabella.

'If my aunts descend you will have plenty to do,' he retorted acidly.

12

It was nearly three weeks since Barbara Lythmore had received a visit from the Marquis of Ullenwood. That was not unusual, for in the six months of their liaison she had found him a careless lover: if he had not been quite so generous she would have been tempted to look elsewhere. But he was exceptionally generous, and when he did not respond to her latest letter, she decided it was time to go in search of him.

Lady Plemstall's parties were always glittering, crowded affairs, where one could expect to see the world and his wife on display, but when Mrs Lythmore arrived at Plemstall House she looked in vain for Lord Ullenwood. She was greeted with smiles and bows from several gentlemen as she crossed the crowded ballroom, received merely a frosty nod from one or two fashionable matrons and no acknowledgement at all from the highest sticklers. She paid them no heed and made her way to the card-room. She paused in the doorway and surveyed the players.

'I fear, madam, that you are to be disappointed tonight.'

The rasping voice in her ear made her step away a little, and she looked round to find a gentleman with badly powdered red hair standing beside her.

'Mr Granthorpe.' She curtsied. 'I have only this moment arrived, sir and always like to know who is present.'

'There is one man you will not find here this evening.' His lip curled into a unpleasant smile.

She tried to ignore it.

'Oh? I have no idea who you mean, for I came with no expectations to meet anyone this evening.'

'Did you not? I thought you looked upon a certain gentleman as your personal property.'

'You talk in riddles, Granthorpe.' She hunched one white shoulder. 'It shows a lack of polish, you know.'

He flushed, and leaned towards her.

'I may lack polish, but if I was to be married in the morning I would make sure my mistress knew of it beforehand.'

Startled, she dropped her fan. Mr Granthorpe bent to retrieve it.

'Yes,' he drawled. 'I thought that would get your attention.'

'What are you talking about?'

'Ullenwood is getting hitched tomorrow, at St George's.'

'That's a lie!' she hissed, her face growing pale beneath her white powder.

'Is it?' he sneered. 'Then explain to me why his coachman was in the Running Footman last night, telling his cronies that he was driving his master to France tomorrow, immediately after the wedding breakfast?'

She snatched her fan from his hand and snapped it open.

'A likely tale,' she said, fanning herself vigorously. 'You have been sold a dummy, sir.'

'Aye, so I would have thought, if I had not heard it for myself.'

It was the lady's turn to curl her lip.

'Ah, yes. I had forgotten your predilection for gin-houses. It is a fashion, is it not, for a gentleman to dress like the driver of a common stagecoach and mix with the scaff and raff.'

He shrugged.

'Sometimes it yields useful information, as in this case, but if you do not believe me, go to Hanover Square tomorrow morning and see for yourself.'

* * *

On her wedding day, Rosamond awoke to a grey, leaden sky and blustery winds that buffeted the carriage as they drove the short distance to Hanover Square. Lord Ullenwood and his secretary had arranged everything for the wedding, leaving Rosamond with little to do, and an odd sense of detachment about the proceedings. The ceremony itself was simple with very few guests, all of them acquaintances of the marquis. She recognized only Mr Mellor who was acting as Lord Ullenwood's groomsman, Lady Padiham and Mrs Tomlinson. As they left the church, a sudden gust of wind hurled icy rain into the portico and the marquis hurried her down the steps to the waiting carriage. As she climbed inside she heard a soft, female voice calling to Lord Ullenwood.

Rosamond turned and looked out. From the shadowy interior of the carriage she watched as a fashionably dressed lady in a powder-blue pelisse trimmed with fur approached. Guinea-gold curls peeped from the edge of a bonnet whose feathery plumes defied the wind and curled down to provide the perfect frame for an exquisite countenance. She moved forward, smiling and extended a hand towards the marquis.

'Elliot, what a pleasant surprise.'

The marquis stood with one hand on the carriage door, observing the speaker impassively. Rosamond noticed that he made no move to take the hand held out to him and after a moment the woman tucked it back inside her fur muff.

'Well, my lord, are you not going to introduce me?' she said, directing a quick glance towards the carriage.

'No, Barbara, I am not.'

Rosamond blinked. The marquis was smiling, but there was no mistaking the implacable note in his voice.

Barbara. Rosamond's suspicions were confirmed: so this was the notorious Mrs Lythmore, Ullenwood's mistress. Rosamond regarded her with interest.

Mrs Lythmore was a renowned beauty and there could be no denying that she presented a very agreeable picture, but unlike Lord Northby's mistress, who had been a little coarse but very kind-hearted, Rosamond thought there was hardness about Mrs Lythmore's mouth, and a calculating look in those cerulean blue eyes. She noted something else, too, as the lady heard Lord Ullenwood's reply: a flash of fury. It was gone in an instant and the widow gave a tinkling laugh.

'Ah, I understand. I intrude upon your day, do I not? How foolish of me, but then, if I had known . . . ' She let the words hang delicately for a moment before giving the marquis another smile, this time (to

Rosamond's mind, at least) full of invitation. '*Au revoir*, my lord.'

She swept away, and the marquis climbed into the carriage. As the carriage began to move, Rosamond could not remain silent.

'Why would you not introduce us, my lord?'

'She is not worth your attention, my dear.'

'But she clearly knows you, sir,' she challenged him, and immediately wondered if she had gone too far.

'I have many acquaintances that I would not wish to introduce to my wife,' he said shortly. 'We shall not speak of it again, if you please.'

Rosamond turned her head to look out of the window. Of course he would not discuss his mistress with her: if he had taken her to wife with expressions of devotion then perhaps there would have been some excuse for the anger and hurt she now felt. She blinked rapidly. This was an inauspicious start to their marriage.

13

The newly married couple returned to Ullenwood House for the wedding breakfast and they visited Sir James before departing for France. They found him sitting up in bed surrounded by papers and books.

'So you are leaving me,' he greeted them jovially. 'Traitors.'

'Careful, James, or I shall cancel my plans. March is not the best of months to journey to Paris.'

Sir James reached out and gripped his hand.

'I know, old friend, and I am very grateful to you,' he said, suddenly serious. 'And to your lady too, for agreeing to go with you. I am much in your debt, ma'am. Well, off you go. The sawbones says I must keep to my bed for another week at least, but by the time you come back I hope I shall be up and about again — I might even have gone back to my own house.'

'You must take as much time as you need, sir,' said Rosamond. 'We were very pleased we could help you and you are no trouble at all.'

He grinned at her.

'My wife takes too much upon herself, James,' growled the marquis. 'You are a damned nuisance. But I don't want your death on my conscience, so you had best stay here a little longer.'

'Thank you, Elliot. *Au revoir*, then. I wish you a safe journey, and an enjoyable one.'

The marquis grinned.

'Of course it will be enjoyable,' he said, 'I am going on my honeymoon!'

* * *

Dover. Rosamond looked out of the window at the expanse of heaving grey water and shivered. A curtain of rain moved across the sea, and occasionally a sudden gust of wind would send it spattering against the glass in front of her. All she had gone through during the last few months had not frightened her as much as setting foot on board the packet for France. For her honeymoon.

Looking out at the restless sea, Rosamond gave a sigh that had nothing to do with the dismal prospect outside the window. Except for a chaste kiss after the ceremony, her new husband treated her very much as he had done before the wedding. He had even been at pains to make sure Henry reserved them separate rooms at Dover, in case they were obliged to wait for a favourable tide.

Fearing she was entering her marriage as a total innocent, Arabella had taken Rosamond aside and explained to her in colourful detail the delights of the marriage bed. Rosamond had blanched at the very thought of a man kissing her, let alone anything more intimate, but Arabella had insisted that sharing a bed with a husband could be a most rewarding experience. Rosamond had stored all this knowledge away, determined to be a good wife, but, as they began the long journey to Dover, the marquis had apologized for rushing her into a marriage, and promised that they should take time to become better acquainted before he forced on her anything other than his name. Rosamond would have found this forbearance admirable if she had not seen the exquisite Mrs Lythmore. Rosamond did not consider herself a vain person, she knew that with her dark, waif-like appearance she would never turn heads when she entered a room, but it was still very lowering to know that the marquis found her so unattractive that he could not bring himself even to touch her.

* * *

The sound of the door opening broke through her reverie. She turned to see Lord Ullenwood come in.

'The captain says the storm is easing,' he said, taking off his caped greatcoat and draping it over a chair before the fire. 'He hopes we shall be able to sail tonight.'

'Then I should tell Meggie not to unpack — '

He put up his hand.

'No need. Davis was on the stairs when I came in. He will tell her.'

'And your coachman?'

'John is already on the quay, overseeing the dismantling of the carriage.' He went to the table and picked up the wine bottle.

'So you see, there is nothing for us to do but wait. Will you take a glass of wine with me, my dear?'

'Yes, thank you.'

'You are very pale.'

She tried to smile.

'I admit I am a little frightened. I had never seen the sea before today.'

'And now I am asking you to sail upon it in the dead of night. I am sorry.'

He came to stand before her, holding out a glass.

She took it, looking fleetingly up into his face.

'Pray do not be. The sooner this part of the journey is over the better. And I am sure there is nothing to worry about: people make this crossing all the time.'

'Bravo, little one.'

She was warmed by his approval, but tried not to show it.

'Besides,' she continued, 'Meggie is far more frightened than I am, so I must set her a good example.'

⋆ ⋆ ⋆

Later, when the party left the shelter of the inn, Rosamond was relieved that the rain had stopped, but the wind was still gusting around the buildings and she had to raise her voice to be heard above the hiss of the waves on the shingle bank.

'How long will the crossing last, do you think, sir?'

'Upwards of three hours, depending upon the wind and the tide,' he replied. 'It has been known for travellers to wait more than a week for a favourable wind. We are fortunate to be away so quickly.'

'Fortunate,' snorted Meggie, walking close behind them. 'Madness I calls it. To be setting off on such a stormy night, and as black as pitch, too.'

A sailor was tossing bundles wrapped in oilcloth on to the deck, but at these words he turned and gave a rasping laugh.

'Lord love 'ee, missus. This ain't dark. They rain clouds is breaking up, see, so we shall have a fair bit o' moonlight to show us the way.'

The maid ignored this well-meant interruption and continued to mutter as she followed her mistress on board.

Several well-placed lanterns illuminated the deck but Rosamond did not know whether to be thankful or sorry that the enveloping darkness hid from them the sight of the water. She could hear it, the waves slapping against the wooden hull, and she could feel it, for the deck moved alarmingly beneath her feet. She clung to Lord Ullenwood's arm as they followed the captain across the deck. He led them down the narrow, ladder-like steps to the cabins, where he opened one door and stood back.

'If your ladyship would like to rest here, and my lord, there is a cabin for you and your valet this way . . . '

'Heaven help us, 'tis a floating coffin!' exclaimed Meggie, following her mistress into the cabin.

'Nonsense,' said Rosamond in bracing accents. 'It is a very practical room.'

A lantern had been suspended from a hook in the ceiling and by its feeble, shifting light Rosamond inspected her quarters. The walls and ceiling were lined in a dark wood and a narrow bed was built against one wall with a small cupboard to one side, holding a metal ewer and a basin. Rosamond's portmanteau had been placed on the floor. She gave a little cry of relief.

'Thank heavens. I have ginger and lemons in there, Meggie. There must be a galley somewhere on this ship: do go and see if you can find a little hot water and I can make us both a warm drink. Mrs Trimble told me that a tisane is very good for settling the stomach.'

Even as she spoke the roll of the ship became more pronounced and Meggie cast her eyes heavenwards.

'I do not see that anything will help us if this gets much worse.'

'Of course it will get worse,' snapped Rosamond, her own nerves fraying. 'We are not yet at sea. Now go and do as you are bid.'

* * *

Alone in the little cabin, Rosamond sat down on the edge of the bed and tried to fight down her fear. She told herself there was nothing to be afraid of. Hundreds, no thousands of people went to sea; many ladies like herself now went on the Grand Tour, so they must all have experienced just such a crossing as this. Once she was used to the rocking motion she was sure she would find it quite soothing. There were muted shouts from the deck, the scrape of metal upon metal and a sudden increase in the movement of the ship beneath her. She gripped the edge of the bed. They were putting out to sea. The lantern swayed wildly and the moving shadows added to her sense of panic. She would have preferred to be outside in the air, but the captain had asked that they stay below deck until they were safely on their way.

Rosamond sat very still, allowing herself to move with the ship. Tentatively she let go of the bed and untied her bonnet and cloak, then she risked standing up to hang them from a hook on the wall. Encouraged by this achievement, she took another look at the cabin. The bed was very narrow, barely wide enough for Meggie's ample form. She knew that a harsher mistress would insist upon her maid sleeping on the floor, but the narrow strip of bare boards between the bed and the wall was scarcely wide enough to walk upon. They must take it in turns to lie down, she thought, or they could sit up, and trust that the crossing would not be a long one.

* * *

Rosamond lay down upon the bed to wait for Meggie's return. Gradually the ship settled into a gentle, steady motion, the activity on the deck ceased and there was only the creaking of the ship's timbers to disturb the silence of the little cabin. Rosamond was beginning to grow concerned for her maid when she heard familiar heavy footsteps approaching and Meggie came in.

'At last. I thought you had fallen overboard.' Rosamond sat up. 'Did you bring some hot water?'

Meggie held up a jug in one shaking hand, her eyes wide and glazed.

'Yes'm, but — ooh miss, I do feel queer!'

* * *

Struggling up on to the deck an hour later, Rosamond clung on to the deck rail and looked about her. A scattering of grey clouds scudded across the paler grey-blue sky, their edges tinged with light from the half-moon. Below her and in every direction the sea was a constantly shifting mix of grey and black with occasional splashes of white on the wave crests. The icy wind stung her cheeks and she threw back her head, revelling in the feel of the biting, salty air on her skin. The huge sails snapped and fluttered above her, and in the centre of the deck stood the black bulk of the Ullenwood travelling carriage, securely lashed to the deck.

She jumped as a figure detached itself from the shadows.

'Are you ill, madam, can I be of assistance?' The marquis came towards her. His face was in shadow but she could hear the concern in his voice.

'No, I am very well, thank you. I came up for a little air.' She saw the gleam of his teeth. He was grinning at her.

'Well, there is certainly plenty of it.' He came to stand beside her, gazing out over the water. 'It has a certain beauty, does it not?'

'Yes. It is exciting, but a little frightening, too. It is so vast. I feel very small, very vulnerable.'

'Would you not be happier in your cabin?'

'I would, perhaps,' she said, 'but my maid is indisposed, poor thing. She is suffering quite dreadfully. I have given her a little lemon and ginger in hot water, and she is sleeping now.'

'Ah. I see.'

'I shouldn't think you do,' she retorted. 'I have spent the past hour ministering to the poor girl.'

‘But I do understand,’ he said, amusement rippling through his voice. ‘You see, Davis has been — ah — similarly affected.’

She stared at him and he nodded.

‘It is true, my dear. My man was taken ill almost before we left port and is now laid out in the cabin, unable to move.’

Rosamond tried hard, but she could not suppress a gurgle of laughter.

‘Oh dear, poor Davis. Should I take him some lemon and ginger, perhaps?’

‘I have already given him brandy, which I think will suit him better than your more wholesome mixture.’

‘It is very cruel of me to laugh, I am sorry. But should you be with him?’

‘I most certainly should not,’ he retorted. ‘He would not thank me for it. He would prefer me not to witness his frailty.’

‘Meggie is just the same. She thinks it most unnatural that I should wait on her.’

‘Then let us consider instead what we are to do for the remainder of the journey.’

Rosamond was philosophical.

‘We must hope the crossing will not be of long duration.’

‘I fear it will be several hours yet.’

‘Oh.’

‘You sound anxious.’

‘Well, yes, I am. A little.’

'We should try to rest.' He held out his hand to her. 'Come along.'

She took it without hesitation.

'Where are we going, my lord?'

'To find a place where we can be comfortable.'

He led her past the crates and the carriage that formed a black mountain on the deck and on towards the stern, where a mass of dark bundles were stacked.

'Fleeces,' he said, leading her towards them. 'British wool is still prized in France.' He threw himself down amongst the fleeces and held out his arms to her.

'Well, madam wife, you had best sit on my lap, and I will wrap us both in my cloak.'

Nervously Rosamond sat down across his knees, and he pulled her against him until her head was resting on his chest. She drew a breath and was aware of the faint rancid smell of the fleeces around them. He wrapped his heavy cloak around them both.

'I must not allow you to catch a chill,' he murmured, his mouth against her hair.

She leaned against him and tried to relax. She had never been so close to any man before, but strangely, she thought she had never felt so safe and warm in all her life. His arms tightened around her.

'Are you comfortable, Rose?'

Oh yes, she thought.

'Thank you, yes,' she said, listening to the steady beat of his heart. 'I have never travelled so far from home before.' She lay quiet for a moment. 'I do hope Sir James will not try to walk too soon. His leg is still not strong. I fear, sir, that without you there to restrain him he will attempt to do too much.'

'He has his man to look after him. You must not be concerned for James: he may seem a frippery fellow, but he is really very sensible, you know.'

'I do hope so. The doctor promised to look in tomorrow — today — to change the dressing on his leg. He must prevail upon him to remain in his bed for some time yet.'

She heard him chuckle.

'I vow you are a born nurse, my dear.'

'I looked after Mama when she was ill.'

'You nursed her until she died?'

'Oh no: that was a fever. Mama and Papa both caught it and I was not allowed to go near them. But Mama had never enjoyed good health — I believe she became ill when I was born and never really recovered. That was why I was sent off to school. Papa could not look after me and applied to my grandfather, who paid for my education.'

'Ah yes, your *excellent* education.'

'Yes, it *was* excellent. Miss Troughton held

very advanced views on female education. She considered our intellect in every way equal to man's.'

'Good God! Did your grandfather approve of this?'

She chuckled. 'Grandpapa did not know of it. He was satisfied that I was doing well at school and never enquired too closely into what I was learning.'

'And your lessons included Miss Wollestonecraft's doctrines?'

'Well, yes, as well as Latin and Greek. Everything that a young man learns at school.'

'Hence your assertion that you could support yourself.'

She sat up.

'And I *could*, if only — '

'If only?' he prompted her, amusement in his rich voice.

She scowled at him, although she doubted if he could see it in the darkness.

'If only gentlemen would not try to seduce me!'

He laughed gently and pulled her back against him.

'Unfortunately, my dear, that is what happens to pretty young ladies,' he said, yawning.

She sat up again.

'Oh. Do you think I am?' she asked shyly.

'What?'

'Do you think I am pretty?'

Peering, she could see that his eyes were closed.

'You have a certain charm.'

'But not enough,' she sighed.

He opened his eyes.

'What do you mean by that?'

'That I am not pretty enough for you to want to seduce me,' she said, greatly daring.

There was silence. Rosamond held her breath, wondering if she had angered him. At last he said quietly, 'I have no need to seduce you. You are my wife.'

'But — '

'Rose, do you intend to talk all the way to Calais?'

'No, but — '

His arms tightened around her, pulling her against him once more.

'Then pray lie still and be quiet, for we both need to rest. We have a long journey ahead of us.'

With a sigh she allowed herself to rest against him while he pulled the cloak around them, tucking it snugly to fend off the chill wind. She rested her head on his shoulder and closed her eyes. She was comfortable and warm, cocooned against the marquis and rocked gently by the movement of the ship.

She listened to the creaking of the timber and the gentle splash of the waves against the hull, breathed in the pleasant tangy smell of soap from the marquis's skin and wool from his coat. So many sensations she wanted to remember. The marquis shifted his position slightly, and he turned his head to plant a kiss on her hair.

'And when I do seduce you,' he murmured, 'it will not be on a noisome packet.'

Rosamond's eyes flew open, but she did not move. The marquis did not speak again and, smiling, Rosamond drifted off to sleep.

14

The rain held off and Rosamond slept fitfully. Whenever she awoke she remained very still, afraid that this idyllic interlude would end. Once, when she had drifted off to sleep, something disturbed her and she jumped. Immediately those strong arms tightened about her and she felt his lips on her hair.

'Hush, love,' he murmured. 'You are safe.'

And Rosamond relaxed again, comforted.

* * *

She awoke when the noise and bustle of the upper decks pierced her consciousness. It was still dark, but a grey light on the horizon ahead of the ship told her that the day was fast approaching. A sudden realization of her position made her grow hot with embarrassment. She eased herself from the marquis's knees but the movement woke her husband. His arms held her firm.

'Trying to escape me, Rose?'

'No, sir. I do not want to burden you.'

'You are as light as thistledown,' he said. 'You will never be a burden to me.'

'Oh, what a lovely thing to say.' She smiled up at him, but her breath caught in her throat as she looked into his face. There was something predatory about his smile, the slant of his grey eyes, dark and hard as slate. Even as her brows drew together the look was gone. He almost thrust her away from him.

'It will soon be dawn. We should return to the lower deck and look to the health of our servants.'

It was what Rosamond had been about to suggest, but now it did not suit her that the marquis should think of it. She felt cheated. Stifling her vague feelings of discontent, Rosamond followed Lord Ullenwood back to the lower deck and made her way to her cabin, where she found Meggie lying upon the bed, pale, but awake and composed.

'Ooh, mistress, have I kept you from your bed? Indeed I could not help it, I felt so bad, miss!'

Rosamond made haste to reassure her, and felt a little guilty that she had enjoyed the crossing so much. The news that land was in sight acted as a powerful tonic on the maid, who was quickly on her feet and anxious to be moving. Rosamond caught her arm.

'Slowly, Meggie. You are still weak. I am told we have an hour or so before we reach the harbour.'

'Then let me pack our bags and prepare, my lady. The time will pass quicker if I am busy.'

They reached Calais just as the first streaks of an icy dawn were stretching across the sky. A small rowing boat came out to take them ashore, where they were escorted to an inn to break their fast while they waited for the packet to dock and their carriage to be unloaded.

By noon they were ready to travel on. The marquis escorted his lady out of the inn. His coachman was waiting, casting a professional eye over the equipage hired to carry the servants and extra baggage.

'It is well built, I have to say,' he remarked to the valet as he supervised the securing of trunks and boxes to the back of the vehicle. 'Of course, this is only a chaise — no driver, you see: only postillions.' The coachman spat. 'Can't hold a candle to my lord's chariot, of course, but with decent nags it will do the job well enough.'

The marquis chuckled.

'Nothing will convince Wilson that his is not the best profession in the world.'

'And so it is, sir,' grinned the coachman, touching his hat. 'King o' the world I am, perched up on the box. Are you ready to be off, my lord? Bags is all packed, you see, so we can be away at your convenience. And I've picked out some rare good 'osses for us.' He used his advantage as a lifelong retainer to wink at his master. 'A few gold coins means the same in any language.'

Rosamond made herself comfortable in the large travelling chariot beside her husband, and glanced out of the window to watch Davis helping Meggie into the second carriage. As the door closed upon the servants she observed for the first time the damaged door panel.

'There was used to be some decoration on the bodywork,' she remarked, frowning. 'I cannot quite make it out, for it has been so badly scratched. How careless to mark such fine paintwork.'

Lord Ullenwood stared at the coach for a moment.

'Not careless, my dear,' he said. 'The coat of arms has been deliberately wiped off. I would wager the vehicle once belonged to some noble family and has been confiscated for the new regime.'

Rosamond turned shocked eyes upon her husband.

'Oh dear. Do — do you think they are . . . dead?' she finished on a whisper.

Lord Ullenwood shrugged.

'Possibly. So many perished in the Terror.'

She sighed. 'It makes it all so much more real. I read the reports at the time, of course, but it meant very little to me then.'

'Try not to let it overset you. It was years ago. France's new consul is now firmly in control, and we are told that France has never been so prosperous.'

Rosamond heard the note of irony in his voice but said nothing, preferring to keep her own counsel.

As they travelled on towards Paris there were many signs that the country was recovering from its revolution. The fields were well tended and the people seemed healthy and happy enough. Women in their red camlet jackets and aprons smiled at them as they passed, but there were also signs of the terrible upheaval the land had suffered: churches with their windows smashed and gravestones knocked down, and through the trees the occasional glimpse of some once-magnificent château now a blackened ruin.

The road to Paris led them through Montreuil, Amiens and Chantilly with its ruined castle. It had seen so many English travellers in the past months that the journey was accomplished in reasonable comfort. With handsome profits to be made, the posting inns were only too happy to offer their best rooms for the rich English milor' and John Wilson had his pick of the horses at each stop, but Rosamond could not be easy. As they neared Paris she stared out of the window, a frown creasing her brow.

'Why so pensive, my dear?'

Lord Ullenwood's words roused her and she forced a smile.

'I am a little apprehensive of Paris, my lord. I am not at all sure that I approve of this new government. On our journey here I have learned that the churches are open again, but the priests are not free to follow their consciences, the newspapers report only what they are told, and Bonaparte has made himself First Consul for life. Our parliament has its faults, sir, but in France it seems the people have no right to say anything against their leader. If we go to the court, will I have to smile and bite my tongue if I disagree with anything that is said?'

'I am afraid that is so, madam.' He smiled at her. 'If it worries you so much, you need not go, I shall not insist upon it. In fact, I would rather you stayed away. I must deliver my messages to the ambassador, and I have promised James that I will do nothing to antagonize the authorities here, but I see no reason to show them more than common civility. After all, they have taken my land, and put kinsmen of mine to the guillotine. I cannot forgive them readily.'

'Then if you will not object, sir, I will absent myself.' She regarded him anxiously. 'As long as it does not jeopardize your position here.'

'No, it will not do that.'

Reassured, Rosamond settled down to enjoy the final stage of their journey. She felt extremely tired, but this was accounted for by the hours of coach travel each day. The inns had been comfortable but not sumptuous, and the marquis had insisted each night that a truckle bed should be set up in her room for her maid. Rosamond knew it was quite usual for married couples to have separate bedchambers, but she found the practice quite disheartening. The marquis had made it plain that their honeymoon would begin once they reached Paris, but, as the days passed and he made no move to do more than kiss her hand, Rosamond's spirits began to droop: she could not believe her husband found her anything but unattractive.

They drove into Paris at the end of a particularly fine spring day, but Rosamond's first view of the city was not encouraging. She disliked the numbers of soldiers on the streets, and shuddered at the sight of the numerous grand houses that stood empty and derelict. She thought there was an air of sadness about the city and the dusty streets made her sneeze. They reached the hôtel Cerutti just as it was growing dark and were shown to their suite by bowing and scraping attendants who assured them that the English milor' had been given the very best and most comfortable rooms in Paris. Milady was called upon to admire the fine gilding on the ceilings, the magnificent reception rooms, and, if one might be permitted, the excellent arrangement of the two main bedchambers with their connecting doors. An excellent arrangement for milord and his new bride, *non*? Rosamond blushed a little at the knowing looks. Now that the travelling was finally over, her head was beginning to ache, and she was relieved when she was left alone with Meggie to change out of her dusty travelling robes and into a fresh grey gown before going back to the elegant salon where a cold supper had been set out for them.

Lord Ullenwood came in, dressed in a tight-fitting black frockcoat and white knee breeches. The severe elegance of his dress caused Rosamond's heart to miss a beat. She thought him the most handsome man she had ever seen. And he was her husband. Lord Ullenwood dismissed the servants and bent an apologetic look upon his bride.

'Would you think me unpardonably impolite if I left you to eat alone?' he said. 'I really think I should see Lord Whitworth as soon as possible.'

Rosamond was surprised to find herself close to tears. She swallowed her disappointment.

'No, of course not, my lord. That is after all the reason we came here.'

He kissed her fingers.

'You are very good. I will conclude my business as quickly as possible, you have my word.'

Rosamond's throat felt very tight.

'You must do your duty.'

He smiled. 'When I return, you shall see how well I do my duty, madam wife!'

Rosamond blushed furiously. With a laugh, Ullenwood flicked her cheek with a careless finger.

'I shall return as soon as I can.'

15

Rosamond had lost her appetite. The little delicacies prepared so carefully by the French chef tasted of nothing. She drank a glass of wine, sent Meggie to hunt out her reading book, and settled down to wait for Lord Ullenwood to return.

Rosamond sneezed. She looked at the gilded ormolu clock on the mantelpiece. Eleven o'clock. It was quite possible that the ambassador had been from home, and Elliot had decided to wait for him. Or perhaps he was entertaining, and the marquis had been obliged to join him, and pay court to a host of French beauties. Rosamond quickly dismissed this disturbing image from her mind. Despite the fire blazing in the hearth she felt very cold, and decided that she might as well go to bed. She sent for Meggie and asked her to warm the sheets before slipping into the filmy nightgown of muslin and lace that Mrs Tomlinson had insisted she should bring with her.

By the time Meggie helped her into bed, Rosamond knew that she had developed a chill. Her throat was sore and her skin felt by turns hot then ice-cold.

'I don't like the look of you, miss. We must make sure you keep nice and warm.'

Meggie shook her head, and went over to bank up the fire.

'I am sure I shall be very well presently,' murmured Rosamond from behind her handkerchief. She leaned back against the soft, snow-white pillows and said with a hint of desperation, 'I cannot be ill now.'

Clucking like a mother hen, Meggie came across to the bed and smoothed out the covers.

'Well, my lady, who knows but what you may be much better by the morning. Perhaps I should have my bed made up in here — '

'No! No, Meggie, I shall do very well: only leave me a cup of lemonade, and my book and my candle.'

After much huffing and puffing the maidservant was at last persuaded to go, and Rosamond was alone. She tried to read, but found her head hurt too much. Gradually the noise from the street died away. She lay back against the pillows, listening for any noise in the house that would herald Lord Ullenwood's return. At last she fell into a fitful doze and awoke some time later with a sneeze.

The adjoining door opened and the marquis entered, carrying a branched candlestick.

Rosamond regarded him with a sleepy gaze. He was wearing a richly patterned dressing gown, the bright colours glaring to her sensitive eyes.

'I saw the light under the door,' he explained, coming towards the bed. 'It is very late, I did not expect you to wait up so long for me.'

'Is it very late?' she murmured, struggling to sit up. 'I did not know . . . I have been asleep.' She sneezed. 'Did you see Lord Whitworth?'

'No. He is out of town for a few days. I must wait for his return.'

'Oh dear.' She sneezed again. 'I am sorry, my lord. I think I have developed a chill.'

'The devil you have!'

He sounded angry, and her spirits plummeted. She retreated behind her handkerchief, tears threatening.

'Pray do not come near me, my lord,' she begged him. 'I may be infectious.'

She heard him laugh.

'You may indeed. Very well, madam wife, I had best leave you to your rest. Goodnight, my dear.'

As the door clicked shut behind him, Rosamond sank down into her bed, thinking herself the most unfortunate wretch in the world.

* * *

Rosamond's illness was violent but short and in three days she felt well enough to sit out of bed for her dinner, and the following morning she joined her husband for breakfast. His welcoming smile cheered her.

'I am relieved to see you out of your room at last,' he said, escorting her to the table. 'I was concerned for you.'

'Yet you never came to see me.'

'Following your instructions, ma'am,' he replied. 'Your maid was adamant that I should not be admitted. You were too ill to bear visitors.'

She gave a rueful smile.

'I think my words to Meggie were that you must not see me looking such a fright! I am sorry, my lord. I never expected her to treat my ramblings quite so seriously. But I have not thanked you for sending up fresh spring flowers to my room every day. They cheered me.'

'I am glad they pleased you, Rose.'

'I trust my absence has not caused offence, my lord. I would not want to make difficulties for you.'

'It is unfortunate that you have had to keep to your room, but we had already agreed that you would not attend the Drawing Room. It was of course necessary that I should do so but having attended once I hope I shall not have to do so again. Lord Whitworth is due to return to Paris tomorrow: I expect him to be at Madame du Taille's salon, and since we have also been invited I shall be able to see him there and hand over Ashby's letter without raising any speculation. However, today I am at your disposal, my dear. I shall devote myself to showing you a little of Paris. Do you feel well enough to go to the Louvre today?'

'Oh yes, Elliot, if you please. I should like that very much.'

Despite her assurances that she was quite well, Rosamond found herself exhausted by the time they returned from the Louvre. The gallery had been hot and overcrowded, and they had been obliged to stop many times for the marquis to make his new bride known to the many English visitors they met. A glance in the mirror upon her return showed her that she was looking grey and wan, and she was grateful when her husband ordered her to take dinner in her room. He kissed her cheek.

'Sleep well, Rose. I would have you in your best looks for your first introduction to Paris Society.'

She went off to her room, her cheek

tingling from the touch of his lips, and it was in a mood of optimism that she prepared to attend Madame du Taille's salon the following day. Meggie might deplore the period of mourning that precluded her buying and wearing the latest French fashions, but secretly Rosamond thought she looked very well in her new white muslin with silver embroidery. Her dark hair was confined by bands of white ribbon and a pair of fine pearl ear-drops and a single string of matching pearls enhanced the flawless skin of her neck and shoulders. 'Well, sir?' she murmured when she joined her husband in the hall. 'Will I do?'

'Admirably.' Her heart soared as he took her silk cloak from the footman and placed it about her shoulders. 'You have never looked better, Rose. Has that maid of yours learned how to dress you at last?'

She gave a gurgle of laughter.

'Yes, Meggie is very impressed by Paris fashions and has taken great pains to make me *à la mode*, despite my being in mourning.'

'So that is another of the dresses you chose with Arabella. You are to be congratulated, it suits you very well.'

'Thank you, my lord. You remind me that I received a letter from Bella today: she tells me that your aunts have yet to descend upon her, but she is very busy keeping Sir James entertained. Is that not good-natured of her?'

'If the choice is between sitting with my aunt Padiham or flirting with James, I do not think it difficult to know which she would prefer.'

Rosamond shook her head at him.

'I think you are too harsh on your cousin. She makes a point of telling me they do *not* flirt: they read together and discuss literature.'

'Good God, pray do not tell me Bella is falling in love with James. He is a confirmed bachelor: it will end in a broken heart. You smile, madam, do you think me wrong?'

'At this distance I prefer to keep an open mind,' she returned primly. 'But they have been thrown together . . . '

'No,' he said decidedly. 'They are too different. It is not logical.'

She stifled a sigh.

'Love is not logical, my lord.'

* * *

As they drove through the city Lord Ullenwood explained to Rosamond that Madame du Taille was one of the most fashionable hostesses in Paris.

'Her salons are always crowded; government ministers, foreign visitors — the world and his wife will be there.'

'I thought we met the world and his wife at the Louvre yesterday,' responded Rosamond, her eyes twinkling. 'But I know so few people; will there be any familiar faces, sir?'

He hesitated for a brief second as the carriage came to a halt.

'No,' he said. 'I think not. We need not stay too long, my dear. I would not have you overtire yourself. Promise me you will inform me when you are ready to leave.'

His concern warmed her.

'I will, sir. You have my word.'

* * *

Rosamond accompanied her husband through a series of large rooms, each one richly decorated in bright colours with sumptuous hangings and an abundance of lavish gilding. Madame du Taille was very gracious and soon carried Rosamond away with her, anxious to introduce the new milady to her guests. When Rosamond met up with her husband some time later, her eyes were shining, and there was a becoming flush to her cheeks. He smiled down at her.

'Well, my lady, are you enjoying yourself?'

'Oh yes, sir. So many people remember my grandfather and were kind to me for his sake,' she told him.

'I think they are kind to you for your own sake, *ma chère*,' put in *madame*. She turned to the marquis. 'I compliment you on your bride, milor'. She is quite charming and her French is impeccable. You should be very proud of her.'

Lord Ullenwood caught Rosamond's fingers and carried them to his lips.

'I am, madam. I think I have made an excellent choice.'

'Do you truly mean that?' Rosamond whispered, her cheeks flushed with pleasure.

'Truly, my little Rose. You have such poise and elegance, I have heard nothing but praise for you. Now, I think our hostess wants to carry you off again.' He lowered his head and whispered, 'I believe she wants to present you to Talleyrand. An objectionable little man, but he is Napoleon's foreign minister and still powerful, Rose. You must be polite to him.'

'I am polite to everyone sir,' she murmured as her hostess drew her away again.

Rosamond happily accompanied *madame* around the room, her spirits soaring from her lord's approval, but an hour later she was growing tired. The rooms were so hot and crowded that her head was beginning to ache. Excusing herself from a lively group of voluble French ladies she went in search of the marquis. The rooms were so full of chattering guests that even with her jewelled heels she found it difficult to see above the crowd and she looked in vain for her husband. She crossed to where the large double doors between two salons had been thrown wide and tried to look for Lord Ullenwood's tall figure.

'My Lady Ullenwood.'

She looked round to see who had spoken and smiled uncertainly as she recognized a familiar face.

'Mr Granthorpe.'

'Your servant, ma'am. You are looking for your husband, perhaps?' he said. 'I think I know where we may find him: I may take you to him?'

Rosamond hesitated. She could not like Mr Granthorpe, and did not want to be beholden to him, but he was holding out his arm to her, offering to guide her to the marquis. What harm could there be in that? She inclined her head and laid her hand on his sleeve.

'Well then, my lady, let me get you through this press.'

He began to lead her across the room. A

momentary gap in the crowd showed Rosamond that they were heading towards the gilded pillars at one end of the room, beyond which were a series of alcoves, possibly originally designed to hold marble statues but now each one was furnished with a small card table and framed with rich brocade drapery. Rosamond's heart clenched suddenly. The curtains were pulled across one of the alcoves, the occupants engaged in a private game of cards, or something more intimate.

She was relieved that Mr Granthorpe was leading her away from the curtained alcove, guiding her through the press of people with a quiet word here and there. Her headache was worsening and she clung to Mr Granthorpe's supporting arm, anxious to reach her husband. The chattering was growing louder, echoing around the high rooms and jarring on her ragged nerves. The crowd seemed to press in upon her, a high wall of silk and velvet.

'Ah, here we are.'

Then, suddenly, the crowd parted, melting back to give Rosamond a view of her husband who was standing just inside one of the alcoves. Rosamond's eager anticipation in finding her husband fled, replaced by aching dismay. Lord Ullenwood was smiling down at the exquisite countenance of Mrs Barbara Lythmore.

* * *

Rosamond wanted to step back, to be swallowed up into the crowd again but Mr Granthorpe held her arm and she could not pull free. An expectant silence had fallen over that corner of the room, everyone seemed to be standing around her, watching and waiting to see how she would react to seeing her husband and his mistress. Rosamond gathered her courage. A quiet word to Mr Granthorpe obliged him to release her and she took a pace forward to stand alone.

She could almost touch the curiosity of those gathered around her. She was sure they all knew that Mrs Lythmore was Ullenwood's mistress. She was also aware of a strong desire to leap upon the widow and scratch out her eyes. Mrs Lythmore had been laughing up at something the marquis had said, but she turned her head, a shade of annoyance passing across her face. If her head had not been aching so much Rosamond might have thought of something to say, but the widow was smiling at her, tucking a note into the marquis's pocket before laying her hand on his sleeve, as though indicating her possession.

'Ah, Lady Ullenwood,' she purred. 'Have you come to take your husband away from . . . us?' she spoke in French, not perfectly but competent, and Rosamond knew the pause was deliberate . . . she might as well have said 'from me'.

The widow's smile grew more malicious. She murmured, 'I wonder if you can?'

Lord Ullenwood opened his mouth to speak but Rosamond forestalled him, forcing a smile to her own dry lips.

'Not only can I do so, but I will, madam,' she said smoothly. 'There are times when only one's husband will do.' Head up, she directed a look at the marquis. 'My lord?'

A gentleman with a shock of untidy hair and an ill-fitting blue frock-coat tittered.

'Yes, do go, milor'. While you are in the room the enchanting Madame Lythmore has eyes for no one else.'

Rosamond's own eyes flashed.

'How unfortunate for the enchanting *madame*.'

Lord Ullenwood stepped up.

'Shall we go, my dear?'

As the marquis escorted her away, Rosamond saw Harry Granthorpe's grinning face and heard the widow's honeyed tones behind her.

'We must let the marquis look after his little bride. I wonder why he took pity on such a pathetic little creature when he could have done so much better for himself.'

Rosamond stiffened, but Lord Ullenwood squeezed her hand.

'You will ignore her, Rose,' he said softly. 'We will not give the tattlemongers any more encouragement. You look tired, my dear. Is that why you came to find me? I shall take you away at once.'

His voice was gentle, but she sensed the annoyance behind the kind words and a grey desolation mingled with her anger. It was not done for a wife to bandy words with a mistress. She should have remained aloof, dignified: pretending she knew nothing of the widow's connection with her husband.

At the door they were obliged to wait while a lackey was sent running for milady's cloak.

'I am sorry my lord, I did not expect — '

'Mrs Lythmore has become the toast of Paris and is to be found everywhere,' he replied. 'She is become quite a favourite of the First Consul.'

'Indeed? Then it would have been better if I had been forewarned,' she retorted. 'Or would you have me believe you did not know she was in Paris?'

'No. I knew she was here.'

Rosamond took a deep breath, swelling with indignation.

'And you did not think it necessary to tell me? I am *your wife*, my lord!'

His frowned at her.

'I need no reminding of that, madam. However, I have already told you Mrs Lythmore is not worthy of your attention.' He looked up. 'Good, the carriage is here.'

He escorted her outside and helped her into the carriage, but he made no move to join her. Turning, she saw him toss a coin to a footman carrying a lighted torch.

'You are not coming with me?'

'No. I have business to conclude here. You will be perfectly safe with John on the box. Wait for me at the hotel, madam. I shall not be long.'

Rosamond stared at him as the carriage pulled away, rage and frustration building until she could stand it no longer, and with a little cry she pummelled the fat squabs of the seat, while hot tears scalded her cheeks.

16

Lord Ullenwood watched the coach disappear into the darkness, then he strode back through the rooms, his height giving the advantage of being able to see his quarry almost as soon as he entered the smaller salon. With a smile and a smooth word he joined the little party conversing with Lord Whitworth, showing no impatience as the ambassador complimented one lady upon her gown, advised another on what to wear to be presented to Napoleon and cheerfully discussed racehorses with a fashionably dressed citizen, whom he introduced to the marquis as Monsieur Miseau, a rising star in the present government.

Compliments were exchanged and when the pleasantries were concluded the marquis was able to draw the ambassador away from the crowd under the pretext of showing him a new snuff-box.

'I have been looking for you all evening,' he murmured.

The ambassador smiled and lifted his eyeglass to inspect the enamelled box the marquis had presented to him.

'I was detained. I believe you called several times while I was away from Paris?'

'Yes. I have a message for you from Sir James Ashby.'

'Ah. I have been expecting such. Give it to me now.' He dropped his handkerchief and as both men bent to retrieve it Lord Ullenwood slipped him the letter.

'Excellent,' remarked Lord Whitworth, returning his attention to the snuffbox. 'An excellent piece, my lord. I do not know when I have seen finer. I shall call upon you, my lord, to see more of your collection. But if you will excuse me, our hostess is beckoning me.'

With a bow and a smile the ambassador walked away. His task completed, Lord Ullenwood eased his way through the crowded salon towards the door, eager to be gone. He thought of Rosamond, returning alone to the hotel. He recalled the distress in her eyes and felt a pang of discomfort, knowing he had been the cause of hurting her. He stopped. There must be no more misunderstandings.

* * *

Turning back into the room, he strode purposefully through the salons until he came to the lively group he was seeking. There was no mistaking the flash of triumph in Barbara Lythmore's eyes when she saw him approaching. She was surrounded by a laughing group of gentlemen, at least two of whom he knew to be ministers of Napoleon's government, but she dismissed them with a smile and turned to greet him.

'You are back so soon, my lord?'

'Yes.' He took her arm and led her to a quiet corner, where they would not be overheard. 'I have returned to do what I should have done before I left England. I was a fool not to make matters plain.'

She patted his arm.

'A new bride must have some attention, Elliot. I admit I wish you had confided in me, but I understand — '

'No, Barbara, I do not think you do. I told you when I arrived in Paris that it is over between us. I told you so again tonight.' He shook his head. 'My error was not to end it before my marriage, but at that time, I thought — '

'You thought your marriage to the nobody would not affect us,' she interrupted, giving him her most alluring smile. 'And you were correct, Elliot. I admit I was angry that you did not tell me, but that was understandable, after all.' She put her fingers against his chest, moving closer to say softly, 'I can forgive that, my lord.'

He removed her hand.

'Your forgiveness is not necessary, madam,' he said coldly. 'By trying to turn you off gently it seems you have not understood. Our liaison is finished.'

She blinked, her smile disappearing for a brief moment but it was soon back in place. She gave a soft laugh.

'What, Elliot? Would you turn me off without a sou?'

His lip curled.

'Those diamonds around your neck cost me a pretty penny. Sell 'em and you will have enough to keep you in comfort for at least a year.'

Her eyes narrowed.

'Why now? What has that little wife of yours said to you?'

'Unlike you, Barbara, she has said nothing, but when you attempted to humiliate her tonight, you went too far.'

'What can that little virgin offer you except novelty, and that will soon wear off, I promise you.'

'Do not sneer, Barbara. It does not suit you.' He stepped away from her. 'When I return to London I shall instruct Mellor to sell the house in Clarges Street. You shall have half the proceeds to, ah, alleviate your disappointment. On no account will you approach my wife again, do I make myself clear?'

Her lips curved into a smile, but it never reached her eyes.

'I think you should be careful how you treat me, Elliot. I am a great favourite here in Paris.'

'With tyrants and regicides? Are you proud of that?'

'I can make life very difficult for you,' she said quietly.

He raised his brows.

'Would you stoop to blackmail now, Barbara? I had thought better of you.'

He held her eyes, his own hard and unyielding as granite. She looked at him resentfully for a moment, then she smiled.

'Come, Elliot, let us part as friends. I should like to think you could call upon me again, should you wish.'

He ignored her outstretched hand.

'No, madam,' he said, his voice icy. 'Your treatment of Lady Ullenwood precludes our future acquaintance.'

With a nod he turned and walked away. As he reached the doors to the salon he heard his name and paused.

'Lord Whitworth. Excuse me, I am about

to take my leave of our hostess.'

'Yes, yes, in a moment.' The ambassador took his arm and led him away from the crowd towards one of the long windows. 'A word of warning before you go. You must be careful, sir. Lady Ullenwood's absence from court has not gone unnoticed. I heard Miseau talking of it to Talleyrand here this evening.'

'Let them talk. My wife has no need to consort with this government.'

'Angry talk, sir, but let me counsel you to keep those sentiments to yourself. The peace is very fragile, and you will need passes signed by Napoleon himself to leave France.'

Lord Ullenwood curbed his anger. He sighed.

'Yes, of course. My apologies, Lord Whitworth: it has been a trying evening. I shall, of course, do all I can to smooth things over, but I will not present my wife at court.'

'Very well. But come yourself to the Drawing Room tomorrow. The First Consul likes to parade his English guests. And after, there are matters to discuss, if you are free.'

'I will be there.' With a curt nod, the marquis strode out of the room.

17

'Your door was locked last night, Rose.'

Lord Ullenwood's voice was very calm, but Rosamond stole a glance at the footman attending their breakfast and wondered if he understood English.

'Yes, sir. I thought it best.'

The marquis dismissed the servant, saying as the door closed behind him, 'Would you mind explaining that to me, my dear?'

Rosamond put down the piece of bread, her appetite gone.

'While our marriage is unconsummated, my lord, it is possible that it can be annulled.'

She dared not look at him, aware that her cheeks were flaming. The stillness in the room was alarming.

'Is that what you want?' he said at last.

'Yes.'

'And may one ask why?'

His tone was perfectly reasonable, but Rosamond trembled.

'It is clear to me that I do not have the — the skills to make you a good wife, sir. Our m-marriage was a mistake, but it is not too late to rectify it.'

'And this is what you want?' he said again. 'Please look at me, my dear. I want the truth.'

Her heart thudding painfully in her chest, Rosamond forced herself to look up.

'Yes,' she said clearly.

'I see.' He reached for a bread roll and began to butter it. Rosamond thought they might have been discussing the weather, so calm was he. 'Does this have anything to do with last night's little contretemps?' he asked without looking up. 'I have told you that you need think no more of Mrs Lythmore. She will not trouble you again.'

But there will be others.

The words remained unspoken, but Rosamond knew she did not want to suffer such agonies again: the searing, stomach-wrenching pain of knowing he was with another woman. Better to end it now.

'Come, my lord. Admit that our marriage was an error of judgement, on both our parts. Better to end it while we can.'

'I am not in the habit of making — ah — errors of judgement,' he retorted coldly. 'However, if that is your final word on the matter then I shall not try to dissuade you. All I would ask is that we keep this decision to ourselves until we return to London.'

'Very well, my lord.'

He rose. 'Good. I am engaged to attend the Drawing Room today, but I have time to escort you to the English Divine, if you would like to go to church?'

Rosamond shook her head, too miserable to speak.

'Then I shall leave you now. Pray do not wait dinner for me: Lord Whitworth wishes to talk privately with me. I shall dine there.'

Rosamond did not move until he had gone out of the room. She listened to his footsteps retreating and only when they had died away did she go to her room, telling Meggie that she had the headache and did not wish to be disturbed.

⋆ ⋆ ⋆

A day and a night alone did nothing to restore Rosamond's spirits, but neither did it weaken her resolve to leave the marquis. She made her way to the breakfast table the following morning prepared for arguments, and was disappointed when Lord Ullenwood greeted her with civil politeness. She sat down and allowed the footman to pour her a cup of scalding coffee, aware of a numbness within. She told herself such gloom was foolish: she had never been on terms of intimacy with her husband, so why should his polite, distant demeanour seem so painful now? She realized with a little start of surprise that it was the absence of hope that was so depressing.

'What say you to a day in the country, my dear?'

Rosamond looked up, surprised.

The marquis continued, 'I would like to visit Château Ullenwood while we are here.'

'But your agent and the lawyers have confirmed there is no possibility of your being able to claim it,' said Rosamond carefully. 'Are you sure it is wise to go back: will it not make you feel the loss even more, if you see it again?'

'Perhaps, but it may also help me to lay old ghosts. I would also like to find our old steward, if he lives. I would like him to know we have not forgotten him. So what do you say, Rose? It is no more than a couple of hours' drive from Paris, and after Bonaparte's outburst yesterday I think it would be best to keep out of the way for a few days.'

'He lost his temper?' she said, diverted. 'Oh how I wish I had been there!'

He laughed. 'I thought you were determined to have nothing to do with this regime?'

'I am, of course, but I am still curious. Will you tell me what happened?'

‘Very well then. It was the usual crowd there, the Russian and Spanish Ambassadors, officials and toadies, and at the centre the First Consul himself, preening and accepting the fulsome compliments that he expects. Then Whitworth came in and Boney went striding up to him and accused him of being bent on war. He ranted for some time, told the assembly that we do not keep our word.’ The marquis scowled. ‘By God, Rose, at that point, I wanted to smash my fist into the little monster’s face, but Whitworth took it all calmly.’

‘He is our ambassador, it is his duty to do so, my lord.’

‘Aye, so it is, but I do not know how he refrained from drawing his sword when Boney was shouting and waving his stick at him, like a madman. Finally, he stormed out, shouting that it is up to the English — the English! — to respect treaties. A fine display of hypocrisy from a man who has used the Peace only for his own ends!’

In the silence that followed, Rosamond watched her husband as he frowned at his cup, caught up in his own thoughts. At length, however, he glanced up, the dark look disappeared and he smiled at her. ‘So, my dear, I am minded to drive out of Paris, to see if the air is any cleaner away from the city.

What do you say?'

Rosamond wondered if the invitation was an olive branch. She nodded.

'I will come with you my lord, and gladly. Only give me a moment to change my dress.'

18

Bright sunshine accompanied Lord and Lady Ullenwood as they drove out of Paris and followed the road towards Chartres.

'Does Wilson know the way, sir?' asked Rosamond as they bowled along.

'I have given him directions. I am informed the house and lands have been split up and sold off. Château Ullenwood will have a new name.'

The journey was accomplished without mishap, and when they stopped to change horses the innkeeper was very desirous that the English milord and his lady should step inside to take refreshment.

'Meggie remarked upon it, and I have to agree I am surprised that everyone we meet is so friendly and obliging,' murmured Rosamond as they drove away from the inn, their host smiling and bowing until they were out of sight.

'And so they are: only too willing to take our money.'

'You are too cynical, my lord.'

'And you are too trusting, my lady.'

She smiled, but refused to argue the matter

and settled down instead to enjoy the drive. Just south of Rambouillet they turned off the main road on to a dirt track that went on for so long the marquis called upon the coachman to stop in order that he could ask directions from an old woman driving geese in the opposite direction. Soon they were on their way again.

'This looks promising,' he muttered when the road began to skirt a high stone wall. 'Yes. Here we are.'

Rosamond saw a pair of stone gateposts ahead of them, each topped with a large stone bird, wings spread, and an enormous, out-of-proportion beak.

'Are they meant to be rooks?' she asked, lips quivering with laughter.

'Of course. Madam, they are part of the Ullenwood coat of arms. It is uncivil of you to mock my heritage.'

'I am sorry. Perhaps French rooks are different.'

He laughed. 'No, you are right. They are dreadfully done.'

The gates were thrown wide, but as the coach turned into the drive it could be seen that they had not been moved for some time, for they were overgrown with grass and brambles. The coachman slowed his team and did his best to avoid the worst of the potholes. Rosamond had no desire to laugh now, and a quick glance at her companion showed that his face was unusually grim. The house, when it came into view, made her gasp.

It had once been a fine country mansion, three storeys high and fronted by a wide stone terrace, but one half of the house had been gutted by fire and stood blackened and forlorn, while the other half was in a poor state of repair, with tiles missing from the high roof, shutters hanging off the windows and the wide, shallow steps leading to the house overgrown with weeds. The coach drew up, and the marquis jumped out. He surveyed the house, making no move to help Rosamond to alight. She climbed down and came to stand beside him and, unable to think of anything to say, she tucked her hand in his arm as a token of her support. He put his hand up to cover her fingers.

'I thought your grandfather's house was in a poor state of repair, but it was nothing compared to this. By God, I think they are using the burned-out section as a cattle shed.'

A burly man in culottes and a leather jerkin appeared around the side of the house and stopped at the sight of them, resting his fists on his hips.

'And who might you be?'

His French was rough, but Rosamond had no difficulty in understanding him, nor his threatening posture. Elliot answered him in his own tongue.

'I was looking for a family that used to reside here. Name of Volages.'

The man spat on the ground.

'They left years ago, when this place was returned to the people. It's mine now.'

His tone implied that he did not welcome visitors.

'Do you have any idea where I might find Monsieur Volages?' asked the marquis.

The man spat again. Elliot reached into his pocket and pulled out a coin.

'Perhaps this will help you remember.'

He tossed the coin towards the man who caught it deftly, looked at it, and nodded.

'Aye. He has a house in Maintenon.'

'Thank you. We will try there.'

A cow ambled out from the blackened arch where massive double doors had once opened on to a grand hallway. Elliot's mouth tightened with disgust and he turned to hand Rosamond back into the coach. He barked an order at his coachman and jumped in beside her as they set off back along the rutted drive.

'Is it far to Maintenon, sir? My lord?'

'What? Oh.' He shrugged. 'No. Not far.'

He sank into the corner of the carriage,

gazing out of the window.

'It must be very distressing to see your property so degraded,' she observed. 'It was a very fine house.'

'Aye, it was. I should be thankful it is a farm now. It would be insupportable to see one of the little tyrant's sycophants in residence. We will go to Maintenon and find Volages. He was a loyal servant, I would see that he has sufficient money. Then we will go back to Paris, pack up and leave for England. I have had enough of this country.'

* * *

They reached the town without mishap, but it took a little time to track down Monsieur Volages, who was living with his married daughter. When he realized who had come to see him he fell on his knees before the marquis, overcome by the occasion.

'Ah, milor', we live in dark times!' he cried. 'For many years we kept the château in good repair for you, living quietly, trying not to attract attention. I was hopeful that I would be able to hold it for you until we were at peace again, but alas it was not to be. Three years ago, the soldiers came, milor', we were turned out. It broke my wife's heart: we came here to live with Suzanne, but she never recovered. She took such pride in the château.'

'I am sure you did all you could, Sebastian.' The marquis spoke quietly, taking the old man by the arm and raising him up.

Rosamond moved away, allowing the marquis and his former servant to talk privately. That the old man was very affected by his former master's visit was plain, and nothing would do for him but that milor' and his lady should come inside and meet his daughter, and they should all take a glass of wine together. Consequently the sun was setting by the time they left Maintenon. The marquis conferred quickly with John Wilson and, as they drove out of the town he explained to Rosamond that they would have to put up at an inn for the night.

'With no moon it would be foolish to attempt the journey back to Paris. John remembers that we passed a respectable-looking hostelry on the way here, the Coq d'Or. Yes, there it is. I trust you will not be too disappointed.'

'No, my lord, I am thankful that we do not travel further tonight. The journey has tired me more than I expected.' Rosamond allowed him to hand her down into the yard, where the red-cheeked landlord with much bowing, begged them to enter his humble property.

Rooms were prepared, a chambermaid appointed to wait upon milady and a substantial supper laid out for them. Rosamond was very tired, but she tried to eat a little, if only to keep her husband company. Lord Ullenwood appeared distracted and she guessed he was thinking of the ruined Château Ullenwood and the people who had lived on the estates, all driven from the land. She ached to take his arm and share his sorrow, but she did not have the right. Her hesitant questions were met with short, curt answers. The marquis could not, or would not confide in her. Disappointed, Rosamond bade him goodnight and retired to her lonely bed.

* * *

A sunny morning did much to restore Rosamond's spirits and she went down to the private parlour set aside for them, determined to be cheerful. She found her husband breaking his fast with a large plate of ham and long, crisp bread rolls that he was washing down with hot coffee and boiled milk.

'Good morning, my lord, I trust you slept well? My bed did not look at all promising, but was surprisingly comfortable. In fact, I think I should have overslept this morning if it had not been for the gooseherd bringing her flock past my window at the crack of dawn.'

He rose and came around the table to hold her chair for her.

'You heard that too? Country ways, my dear. At Leverhill my father always deplored the proximity of the Home Farm to the Hall. If you lived there you would soon grow accustomed to the noise.'

'I am sure I should.' She suppressed the comment that since they had agreed to end their marriage there would be no opportunity for her to visit Wiltshire. The thought gave her no pleasure. 'How soon will we be able to leave Paris and return to England?'

'When we get back today I will begin preparations for our journey. Poor Rose, are you so eager to quit France?'

'On the contrary, my lord. I have not yet had the opportunity to buy the dashy dress that Arabella so desires.'

'Ah.' He nodded. 'An important matter, I see. Well, I do not wish to delay our departure from Paris, but we shall be back in the capital soon after noon today. If John can find you fresh horses then and you are not too tired, you may sally forth to find a gown for my cousin.'

'Do you expect me to complete the operation in a few short hours?' she asked him, her eyes wide. 'Bella will expect me to agonize over the decision for at least a week.'

He met her eyes with a smile in his own.

'From all I have learned about you, Rose, I do not think you will do that.'

Her eyes twinkled.

'Oh, is that not how all females are expected to behave?'

'Not you. I think you are a woman of quite superior sense.'

Rosamond's cheeks grew warm.

'Y-you do?' she stammered.

'Yes. In fact . . . '

Rosamond held her breath, hopeful anticipation growing in her breast, but whatever words the marquis had been about to utter were lost. There were sounds of raised voices outside the door, and the next moment Rosamond's maid burst into the room.

'Oh, madam, thank heaven we have found you!'

Startled, Rosamond jumped up.

'Meggie! Heaven and earth, what is wrong?'

Instead of answering the maid threw herself into her mistress's arms and sobbed loudly.

'Thankfully Davis is here also,' remarked the marquis. 'Perhaps he will enlighten us.'

The valet gave a slight bow. He was pale but appeared perfectly composed. He dismissed the curious servant and shut the door carefully.

'Come and warm yourself by the fire, man,' Lord Ullenwood ordered him. 'You must have been travelling half the night to be here so early.'

'Yes, sir. We were up before dawn.'

Rosamond resumed her seat and drew Meggie down on to a chair beside her.

'Then pray tell us what has prompted such action,' she said.

Davis nodded.

'Of course, ma'am. Last evening, Lord Whitworth himself called at the house. Upon learning that you had not yet returned he asked to speak to me. He said he had come to advise that you should pack up and leave the city immediately.'

'Indeed,' said the marquis. 'Did he give a reason?'

'Aye, sir, eventually,' replied the valet, with a ghost of a smile. 'I doubt he considered it necessary for me to know why he should be advising you thus, but I explained to him that you had gone out of Paris, and, as I did not expect you to return until the morning, I would pack up and follow you out of the city. When he heard that, Lord Whitworth decided to — er — open the budget. Thank you, my lord.' Davis paused as the marquis handed him cup of coffee, and he drank a little before continuing. 'The ambassador says someone has laid information against you, my lord. It is alleged that you arrived here carrying messages harmful to France. Orders have been issued to arrest you and my lady.'

'Oh good heavens!' murmured Rosamond, her hand going to her cheek.

'Aye, ma'am, we was that afraid, I can tell you,' added Meggie, wiping her eyes on her sleeve. 'We began to pack up immediately, ready to leave the city before the soldiers came.'

'We left as soon as it was light, my lord,' explained Davis. 'I told the hired postillions that Lord Whitworth had brought word from Lady Padiham in England, ordering your immediate return. I hoped it would allay their suspicions.'

'A good thought, Davis. Well done.'

The valet drew a folded sheet from his pocket.

'Lord Whitworth also instructed me to give this to you.'

The marquis opened the paper and perused it in silence.

'You have read this?' he said, directing a searching look at Davis.

'No, my lord.'

'Good.'

Lord Ullenwood carried the paper to the fire and pushed it between the logs. Almost immediately the flames leapt around it. Rosamond watched him, frowning.

'Is it bad news, my lord?' she said.

'It is better that no one but myself knows what was written in that note.' He returned. 'You could be accused of spying.'

Three pairs of eyes were fixed on him, but he did not elaborate.

'Come,' he said, 'we must make haste to be away.'

Davis held up his hand.

'One more thing, my lord. The ambassador said the northern ports are being watched. And we cannot turn off the postillions: if they return to Paris they could give evidence of our direction.'

'True. We had best go south towards the coast. Come,' he held his hand out to Rosamond. 'We must make haste to depart now. Davis, pray make it known here that we have been summoned back to England. It will account for our haste.'

* * *

It was a tense hour before they left the inn. Rosamond feared that at any moment the shout would go up, and they would be detained, but at last their carriage rolled out onto the road with Davis and Meggie following behind in the baggage coach.

Rosamond stole a glance at the marquis, who was staring out of the window, a slight frown on his brow.

'Who do you think laid information against us, my lord?'

'I cannot be sure, but I think it might be Barbara Lythmore.'

'I think that too,' she replied. 'If you will permit me to speak plainly, I think she wanted you for herself.'

The marquis shrugged.

'Since we are speaking plainly, then let me apologize to you, my dear. It was remiss of me not to settle with her before I married you.'

'It would have been courteous to inform her of the event,' agreed Rosamond.

'I know. It was arrogant of me not to do so, but I thought she understood our situation: I made it very plain that I would never marry her.'

'Perhaps she hoped to change your mind, my lord.'

'She told me she did not want marriage.'

'Of course she said that: it was what you wanted to hear,' Rosamond retorted. 'Really, men can be so blind at times. I have no doubt she expected her reticence to excite your interest.'

'Is that why you held me off, to increase my desire?' he asked her.

'You have never desired me,' she flashed. 'Ours was a marriage of convenience. Your words, my lord, if you recall.'

'Aye.' He scowled and turned away from her. 'Will you ever let me forget it?'

Rosamond hunched a shoulder and gazed out of the window.

'Aye, sir, when we are free of this sham. Then it will not matter to me how many *billets* your mistress sends you.'

'And what am I to understand by that?'

'Do you think I did not see the notes she sent to you at Ullenwood House?'

He frowned.

'*Then* I was not married, nor even betrothed. I would not countenance such a thing to continue now.'

'Hah!'

He sat up.

'By God, I had no idea I had married such a termagant! What do you mean with your *hah!* madam?'

She turned to face him, her little foot tapping angrily upon the floor, her eyes dark with fury.

'How am I to believe you, when I saw her with my own eyes, slipping a note into your pocket?'

'Impossible.'

'Is it, my lord? When Harry Granthorpe led me up to you at Madame du Taille's, I saw Mrs Lythmore putting a letter into your pocket. *Now* what will you say?'

She waited, but he did not appear to be listening.

'So that was it. By gad, the little vixen — *that* was why she was trying to distract me! Rose, it was not a love note she was giving me: I had Ashby's letter in my coat that night, addressed to Lord Whitworth. Barbara must have been pulling it out of my pocket when you came up, and knowing you had seen her, she pushed it back again.' He gave a harsh laugh. 'What is that line from Congreve, *Heaven has no rage like love to hatred turned, Nor hell a fury like a woman scorned*. Thank heaven she did not steal it from me. I would not hazard a groat that she would not pass it to her new French friends. You are still scowling at me, Rose. Do you not believe me?'

'Yes, I believe you,' she said slowly, 'but to speak against you in a way that could harm you — might even lead to — ' She shuddered. 'It is quite — quite evil. I cannot think of it without abhorrence.'

He reached out and caught her hands.

'Then do not think of it at all! Let us

concentrate on getting out of this damned country.' He squeezed her fingers. 'Come, madam, we could deal much better than this, we *must* do so if we are to escape from this fix. What do you say, shall we cry friends?'

'Yes my lord, if you wish it.'

Rosamond sank back in her corner, watching the fields and trees rolling by. Within her she felt the first tiny flicker of hope.

19

They took the Chartres road and, as they travelled away from the influence of the capital, Rosamond noticed a change in the manner of the local people. There were no cheerful landlords ready to run out and offer their best horses for the English milord and as they bowled along through the open countryside the few labourers they met merely watched them with unfriendly, sullen faces as they drove by. They stopped at a large roadside inn for the night and Rosamond was very aware of the surly attitude of the stable boys. The landlord was civil enough, but when they went out to the coach the following morning, John Wilson was sporting a very colourful eye.

'Had a little falling out with one o' the lads,' he explained when his master remarked upon it. 'He seemed to think England is full o' white-livered ne'er-do-wells, but not to worry, my lord,' he added cheerfully, gathering up the reins, 'I soon put 'im to rights, cheeky young jackanapes.'

'I did not think John a very fiery character,' remarked Rosamond, as they pulled away.

Lord Ullenwood frowned.

'He is not. The provocation must have been great. I fear the news is spreading that the peace will not last.'

'The people certainly do not seem as friendly here. On our route from Calais to Paris everyone was only too happy to see us.'

'They were happy to take our money,' he amended drily. 'Do you still think me too cynical?'

'No,' she sighed. 'I am very much afraid you are right.'

* * *

Another long day's travelling took them past Le Mans and on the road to Rennes, Lord Ullenwood expressing his intention of driving into Brittany before heading to the coast and finding a boat to take them to England.

'But,' Rosamond hesitated, 'do we not need permits or, or papers to leave France?'

He smiled at her.

'We must hope that the locals are amenable to bribes.'

They stopped for the night at a small country inn, where the landlord was inclined to haggle over the cost of providing so many rooms for milord and his entourage.

'I mislike the look of our host,' murmured

the marquis as they were shown into their private parlour. Meggie will share with you tonight. Make sure you keep her with you.'

Rosamond took her chance.

'If it is so dangerous, I would rather have your company, my lord.' She kept her tone light, but she held her breath while she waited for his reply.

Lord Ullenwood regarded her with an amused eye.

'Would you, my dear? I am flattered, of course, but I must not allow you to tempt me: I must keep my wits about me tonight.'

Rosamond turned away, her cheeks burning. He had snubbed her again. She busied herself with removing her cloak while she regained her composure, so that by the time they sat down to supper she could hide her disappointment and converse calmly with him.

* * *

The morning brought another problem. Rosamond went down to the parlour to find Lord Ullenwood already discussing a hearty breakfast. He got up as she entered and came forward to pull out a chair for her.

'Meggie tells me the postillions have fled,' she said without preamble.

'Yes.' He resumed his seat. 'They have taken the hired carriage. We must be thankful that John decided to sleep in the chariot, or we may have lost that, too.'

Rosamond watched him as he poured her a cup of coffee, no sign of anxiety in his face. She struggled to match his cool manner.

'So what do you think we should do, my lord, can we hire another coach?'

'I have asked the landlord, but with no success. He either cannot or will not help us with a carriage, and even if he could provide one, he tells me the postillions will not ride with an English party.'

'Are we so unpopular, then?'

'It would appear so, my dear. You must not worry, Rose. I shall bring you home safe.'

She returned his smile.

'I have every confidence in you, my lord. However, I, too, have been considering our situation. Can we not manage with a single carriage? It might be a little crowded, but not impossible. We would, of course, be obliged to leave behind some of our trunks, I think.'

'Could you do that?'

'Of course, my lord, if it is necessary.'

'Then I think that is what we must do. Meggie shall travel inside with us, Davis can sit up on the box and act as guard.'

She looked up, startled.

'Dear me, are things as bad as that?'

'We are a long way from Paris now. There Napoleon's soldiers keep the peace and enforce his will; here in the country his iron grip is not quite so firm: we must be prepared.'

After an hour repacking the trunks they set off in their one remaining carriage.

'What do you think will become of our baggage?' asked Rosamond, as they drove away from the inn.

The marquis shrugged.

'I told our host that my servants would be back to collect it, but I have no doubt that it will have disappeared by this evening.'

Meggie clutched at the bandbox balanced on her knees.

'Shameful, it is,' she muttered.

Rosamond was more philosophical.

'There is nothing we cannot replace, Megs, once we are back in England.'

'If we get back,' muttered the maid, frowning direfully.

* * *

For the first few hours they journeyed without mishap, but when they stopped for fresh horses at a small country town, several raggedly dressed individuals came to stare at them, muttering under their breath as they regarded the elegant travelling chariot with its coat of arms emblazoned proudly upon the door.

Meggie glanced out of the window and sniffed.

'Never seen such a lot of ill-looking peasants. I hope we are moving soon.'

'Hush, Megs, we are on our way now.'

Rosamond tried to reassure her as they set off again, but as they pulled away one of the men reached down to pull off his shoe and hurl it against the side of the coach.

'Mercy me!' screamed Meggie. 'They are trying to kill us.'

'Nonsense,' returned Rosamond briskly. 'It was only a sabot with a wooden sole. Sit up straight, Meggie and show them we are not afraid of their high spirits.'

Her brave words won her an approving look from the marquis, which raised her own spirits.

The carriage picked up speed and they soon left the town behind them. They made good time for the road was well made, running between acres of brown earth which showed no signs of new spring growth. Rosamond dozed in the corner, trying to catch up on sleep missed during her restless night but a sudden slowing of the pace roused her and she sat up, blinking. Peering through the window, past the driver she could see the road sloped gently down towards a crossroads, where a small crowd was gathered. They looked to be shabbily dressed, some in leather jerkins or dirty smocks and most were carrying pitch-forks or shovels. Lord Ullenwood let down the window and leaned out.

'Whip up the team, John. They will scatter when they see we do not intend to stop. Davis, keep your shotgun ready, but do not fire unless you must.' He closed the window and began to pull down the blind, requesting that Rosamond and Meggie do the same. The carriage picked up speed and thundered down the road, rocking and jolting alarmingly. The shouts of the crowd grew louder, but with the blinds drawn they could only imagine what was happening outside. From the darkened carriage they heard their driver shout out a warning to stand aside. Rosamond bit her lip to stop herself from screaming as thuds and bangs were heard on the carriage. Then the door was yanked open and a rough-looking man was perched on the step, clinging precariously to the door frame.

Meggie screamed and fell back against Rosamond. Elliot leapt forward and smashed his fist into the grinning face. The man fell back on to the road and the marquis leaned out to reach for the door that was swinging wildly. As he did so a shot rang out and with an oath he reeled back. Rosamond thrust Meggie aside and grabbed at Elliot's coat, pulling him on to the seat. Then she stepped past him and grabbed at the door, pulling it closed. All the time the carriage thundered on, the pace never slackening.

'Heaven and earth, he is killed,' cried Meggie. 'They've killed the master!'

'No, he lives.' Rosamond tried to stop herself from shaking. She had to think clearly. 'He lives,' she said again, adding under her breath, 'but I do not know what to do.'

She looked at the marquis, slumped on the seat. She tried to pull him into a more comfortable position and only partially succeeded, but she was relieved when he groaned and opened his eyes.

'Thank God,' she murmured.

He put out his good hand.

'Help me to sit up. What happened?'

'You were shot, I think, when you tried to shut the door.'

With difficulty she struggled to remove his coat, gasping as she pulled it from his injured arm and saw the bright red stain seeping through his jacket.

The marquis regarded his injury with detached interest.

'Peppered with shot, by God.'

'There is nothing to be done until we can stop,' said Rosamond, suddenly decisive. 'I will bind it up for you as best I can until then.' She tugged off the linen fichu from her neck and began to wrap it around his arm, trying not to look at the ragged little holes in the sleeve.

Meggie was shivering in the corner, whimpering to herself. Rosamond ignored her and tried to think what she should do next. The frantic jolting of the carriage had settled into a more rolling motion. She risked putting up one of the blinds. There was no sign of anyone on the road, and she put up the rest of the blinds before opening the window to call to the driver.

'John, John — th-th master is wounded. How soon can we stop?'

She heard the coachman smother an oath then he held a quick conversation with Davis. She clung on, the cold air stinging her cheeks, until John leaned down and shouted at her.

'We'll put a bit more distance between us and that town, m'lady, then we'll stop and Davis'll have a look at the master.'

Rosamond sank back into her seat. She was shaking.

'Oh dear, oh lord, m'lady. Whatever shall we do?' cried Meggie, rocking herself backwards and forwards in the corner.

'Stop it, Megs. You are of no use to me if you are hysterical.' Rosamond knew her tone was sharp, but she was relieved to see the maid sit up a little straighter and wipe her eyes on her sleeve. She turned back to Lord Ullenwood.

'Be still, my lord. We shall soon be able to stop and make you more comfortable.'

'When we do, tell Davis to get the brandy from my trunk.' He struggled to sit up. With relief she found that the carriage was slowing and pulling off the road. Almost as soon as it came to a stand Davis was at the door, his usual impassive countenance pale and anxious.

'How is the master? If you will permit me to come to him, ma'am.'

Rosamond moved out of the coach, pushing her maidservant out before her. They found that John had secured the horses and climbed down from the box. Now he stood anxiously beside Meggie, trying to see what Davis was about within the shadowed body of the coach. At last Davis came back to the door.

'There is lead shot in his arm and shoulder,' he said, his voice cracking a little. 'It must come out, but . . . I cannot do it, not here.'

Rosamond looked past him. Lord Ullenwood was still slumped into one corner, but Davis had removed his coat and torn away the sleeve of his linen shirt to expose the bloodied flesh. She swallowed.

'Give him some brandy, then, if it will dull the pain for him. Then we must find a house to take us in. No matter the cost — ' She broke off in alarm as there came the sound of a horse approaching. John dragged the shotgun from the footwell. Comforted by this show of support, Rosamond walked to the edge of the road. A gig was coming towards her at a very smart pace, the driver and sole occupant a gentleman in a black frockcoat with a fur hat on his head and a woollen muffler wrapped around his neck. As the gig drew closer the driver brought his horse to a stop.

'Good day to you, *madame*.'

Rosamond was encouraged to see he was an elderly gentleman, his voice soft and cultured.

'Is anything amiss, can I be of help?'

'Thank you, sir,' responded Rosamond in her impeccable French. 'We have suffered a mishap, but we would not wish to importune you.'

The old gentleman put up his hand.

'You are English, I think. You need not fear me, *madame*. I am Doctor Sireuil, physican for the village down there in the valley — '

'A doctor!' Rosamond's cool defences vanished. 'Sir, if you would be kind enough to step down and tend my husband. We were waylaid a few miles back . . . '

With surprising agility the old man jumped down.

'Show me.'

Rosamond led him to the carriage where he carried out a swift examination of Lord Ullenwood.

'He needs immediate attention,' he said, stepping down from the carriage. 'My house is less than a mile from here. Tell your coachman to follow me.'

'Sir,' Rosamond stopped him. 'The village we passed through was very hostile to us. Are you sure — '

'*Madame*, I am a doctor. Your husband's wounds must be cleaned and dressed as soon as possible. Every minute we delay increases the risk of infection. Now, will you come?'

'It seems we have no choice, *m'sieur*.'

He fixed her with a pair of grey eyes that were surprisingly understanding.

'Not if you would save your husband, *madame*.'

⋆ ⋆ ⋆

They followed the doctor over the hill and into a small town. The sun had set and inside the carriage it was too dark for Rosamond to see the marquis. Only his stentorian breathing told her he was still alive.

The doctor's house was a square, stone building on the edge of the town. They stopped at the wide oak door and the doctor's servant came out to help Davis and John Wilson carry the marquis into the house. Rosamond followed silently as the marquis was laid on a cold, leather-covered table in the doctor's surgery. She stayed with him while the doctor gave instructions to the servants. Moments later he returned and began to remove his coat.

'I have sent your maid to prepare a room for you, *madame*, and instructed your coachman to drive the coach into the barn next to the house. The people here are very good,' he murmured with an apologetic smile, 'but they would not look kindly upon an English party in their town.' He began to roll up his sleeves. 'My widowed sister lives with me and acts as my housekeeper and assistant, but, alas, she is gone to attend her daughter's lying-in: I regret there is no one to receive you, madame . . . ?'

'Ullenwood,' murmured Rosamond. 'I am Lady Ullenwood.'

The words were unfamiliar on her tongue. Rosamond realized it was the first time she had actually spoken her married name. 'It is *I* who should be apologizing for inconveniencing you, *monsieur*, but in the circumstances I can only be thankful that you came upon us.' Her voice cracked and the doctor patted her arm.

'You must not worry, milady. I have dealt with many such injuries here. It is, after all, farming country, and my neighbours like their sport. But I shall need help and I have asked milor's valet to assist me.' He nodded to Davis as he came into the room.

'Must I go?' Rosamond turned her solemn gaze upon the doctor. 'I have had some little experience of nursing, and I would like to help you, if I may?'

Those kind grey eyes smiled at her.

'But of course, milady. *Alors*, let us begin. Go to your husband, *madame*. I look to you to comfort him, while we work. Courage, *madame*, it is not so bad as it first appears. Much of the shot has not penetrated the skin, merely bruised it, but there are several pieces that we must get out.'

* * *

The doctor made his preparations with calm efficiency, issuing quiet instructions to Davis who began to cut away the remains of Lord

Ullenwood's bloodied shirt. Rosamond stood silently beside the table, where the marquis lay on his back, his ragged breathing the only sign of life in him. She felt so helpless: she had been ordered to look to her husband, who was unconscious, and for the moment did not require her services. Itching to be useful, she could only gaze about the room. It bore witness to its owner's profession, for it was lined with cupboards and shelves upon which books, bottles and jars were neatly stored. The cleanliness and order gave Rosamond some confidence, and although she found herself growing cold when Dr Sireuil opened a large leather case and began to take out a selection of lethal looking instruments, she was impatient for him to begin removing the tiny pieces of shot. She looked down to find the marquis had opened his eyes and was watching her. He put up his good hand and she caught it, holding his fingers against her breast.

'Where am I?'

'The good doctor has brought you to his house, my lord.'

'Ah, milor' is awake,' said the doctor, rolling up his sleeves. 'I suggest, milady, that you give him more brandy, as much as he will take. He will then feel less pain.'

'The devil I will!' muttered Lord Ullenwood.

Rosamond picked up the cup.

'Come, sir, it will make you more comfortable.' She helped the marquis to drink. Then she refilled the cup.

'Madam, I will not be responsible for my language if you force me to drink all that.'

She allowed herself a small smile. 'I will gladly suffer a few oaths if it saves you some pain, sir.'

* * *

While Davis held Lord Ullenwood steady, the doctor cleaned his arm and began the tortuously slow process of removing the shot. Rosamond remained beside the marquis, holding his hand and occasionally wiping his face with a damp cloth. Each time the doctor prodded and probed, the marquis gripped at her fingers, muttering an apology, but as the brandy infected his brain his civil remarks were replaced by invective and a string of oaths that made the doctor chuckle.

'Bravo, *m'sieur*. You swear as mightily as any Frenchman!'

Watching his ashen face, Rosamond realized that the marquis had gone beyond reason now, and he began to thrash around, trying to get up. She and Davis struggled to restrain him, and she was about to suggest they call for more help when he suddenly stopped moving.

'Do not look so alarmed, milady, he has merely fainted,' murmured the doctor. 'It is best. *Vite*, let us get on while he feels no pain.'

Rosamond risked a brief glance at the wounded arm. Where the flesh was not lacerated and bloody it was already showing dark bruising. She quickly looked away, stifling a shudder. Rosamond made herself as useful as she could, replacing guttering candles, keeping the fire blazing and searching out the bandages that the doctor told her he would need soon to bind up the wounds. When she could do no more, she dropped into a chair to watch the doctor continue his painstaking work. The blinds had been drawn against the icy night and a kettle suspended at the edge of a blazing fire sang quietly. Rosamond dozed.

* * *

'*Voilá. C'est finis.*' Dr Sireuil stood back. 'I have spread balsam on the wounds. Now we will bind him up and move him to a bed, where he may rest. Then he is in the hands of the Lord.'

Rosamond jumped up and brought over

the bandages. She admired the efficient way the doctor wrapped the bandages tightly around the arm and shoulder. She wondered what the old man would say if she confessed that this was the first time she had seen her husband's naked torso. Indeed, she had never been this close to naked male flesh before and she had to force herself not to blush and tremble as they stripped the marquis and put him into a clean nightgown before calling for the servant to help carry him to the bed.

The bedchamber prepared for them was large and welcoming. Candles glowed in their wall sockets and a cheerful fire crackled in the hearth. Meggie had turned down the bed and now she helped Davis and the servants to lay their burden gently between the sheets while Rosamond merely looked on. Dr Sireuil touched her arm.

'You are tired, *madame*. Your maid is waiting for you in the next room. I will sit with milor' while you sleep.'

'No, I would like to stay here. You too must be tired, sir: you have not rested since we arrived.'

'Very well, if you are sure. I shall sleep, but I will be with you in an instant if you need me. You need only send a servant.'

'You are very good.'

The doctor left the room, shutting the door

quietly behind him. Rosamond sat down on a chair by the bed. She watched the valet straightening the covers.

'He drank a lot of brandy,' she said, 'I fear he will have a fearsome headache when he wakes.'

'Not he, my lady. The master has a strong head, and a strong heart, too. He will come through this, never fear.'

'I pray you are right. You were very calm when you were helping the doctor. You have dealt with such wounds before?'

The valet allowed himself the ghost of a smile.

'I have been with my lord since he was a boy, ma'am. Not always as peaceful as these last few years in England.'

She sighed.

'I have known Lord Ullenwood such a short time. There is so much to learn.'

'But well worth the trouble, ma'am, if I may say so.' Davis hesitated. 'The master is a proud man, my lady,' he said, choosing his words with care. 'He was never one to wear his heart on his sleeve, as the saying goes. And some say he is too inclined to keep his own counsel. But he can be kind, ma'am: he has never yet betrayed my trust, and we've been through a few scrapes together, believe me.'

'You are very fond of your master, I think.'

'Why yes, ma'am. A man couldn't ask for a better master: I wouldn't give him up lightly.'

Rosamond felt the tears prickling behind her eyes and was obliged to blink rapidly.

After a moment Davis continued, 'The master should sleep for a few hours yet, ma'am, and if you are wishful to stay with him, then, with your permission, I will retire to my bed and relieve you in the morning.'

'Yes, thank you, Davis.'

'Goodnight, my lady.'

The valet withdrew, and Rosamond was alone with Lord Ullenwood. She pulled the chair closer to the bed and sat down. The house grew quiet and there was not even the ticking of a clock in the room to break the silence. With nothing to do, the hours dragged by. Rosamond paced around the bed, touching the unfamiliar furniture, peering at the dark paintings on the wall before going back to the bed. The marquis had not stirred, and she reached out a trembling hand to lay it on his neck, feeling for a pulse. Reassured, she watched him sleeping for a few moments, then went across to build up the fire. As the hour advanced she grew sleepy. The only chair in the room was wooden and spindle-backed; she could not rest there. She looked at her husband, sleeping peacefully in the big bed. With a little shrug she turned down the lamp and climbed up on the bed and pulled the coverlet over her. Now, lying beside the marquis, she was aware of his regular breathing. She moved a little closer. She was still fully clothed, and there were several layers of blankets between them, but she measured her length against her husband and inched closer until her head was touching his good shoulder. Within seconds she was asleep.

* * *

Rosamond awoke instantly when Lord Ullenwood stirred. She raised herself on one elbow.

'My lord? Are you in pain?'

'Thirsty.'

It was only a whisper, but Rosamond slipped from the bed and hurried around to the table, where she picked up the cup and held it to his lips, her other hand gently supporting his head. He sank back again, his breath hissing through clenched teeth.

'Shall I call Dr Sireuil?'

'No, it was the movement. I shall be fine if I lie still. Come back to bed.'

'I beg your pardon?'

He looked at her, a hint of a gleam in his eyes.

'You were sleeping beside me.'

'I — '

'Come back. Please.'

Awkwardly she climbed upon the bed again and lay down.

'You were much closer.'

'I fear I will disturb you, my lord.'

He reached out his good hand and found hers, lacing his fingers through her own.

'I want to know you are near me,' he muttered sleepily.

20

When Rosamond woke again the sun was shining, filtering around the edge of the thick curtains. It was very quiet and she lay still, wondering what had woken her: she heard a soft click and glanced towards the closed door. Her face flamed. She was still lying under the coverlet with her fingers entwined with those of her husband. If Davis had come in — she broke off, laughing at her naivety. She was confident that Davis was privy to most of his master's secrets and as much to be trusted as her own dear Meggie.

She slipped from the bed, shook out her skirts and went to the door. Davis was coming up the stairs with a jug of hot water.

'Good morning, my lady. I have taken the liberty of ordering hot water to be taken to your room: you may leave the master to my care now, if you please.'

'Thank you, Davis.'

His tone and countenance were as impassive as ever, but she was convinced he had entered the bedchamber and seen her sleeping with the marquis.

* * *

Rosamond returned to Lord Ullenwood's room as soon as she had changed her crumpled gown and taken breakfast. She found the doctor had already made his examination and declared himself satisfied that his patient's wounds were healing well. Rosamond looked doubtfully at the pale, still form in the bed.

'I have given him another sleeping draught,' Dr Sireuil explained, observing her frown. 'He needs to rest as much as he can.'

'What can I do?' she asked him.

The old man shook his head.

'Watch and pray, madam. Watch and pray.'

* * *

The days settled into a familiar pattern with the little party taking turns to keep watch at Lord Ullenwood's bedside; even John begged to be allowed to join in, rather than kicking his heels all day in the doctor's kitchen. It was agreed that John and Meggie would share the night watch, with Davis in attendance upon his master for most of the day. Rosamond sat with her husband as often as she could, but Davis would politely drive her away whenever the doctor came in to examine the marquis and he would not allow her to help change the dressings or perform any little service.

'You must save your strength, ma'am,' he told her, ushering her out of the room. 'My lord knows not who is by him at present: when he comes to his senses, then he will want you with him and you must be ready.'

* * *

So Rosamond went away and filled her spare hours helping where she could around the house. She was soon on excellent terms with the doctor and laughed at him when he exclaimed that milady should not be mending sheets.

'Why not?' she countered, re-threading her needle. 'It will be one less task for your sister when she returns. Have you heard from her?'

'Yes, she tells me her daughter is very weak following the birth and she will be needed there for a few more weeks yet.'

'Then I am happy to be able to help you here, and besides I must do something to earn my keep. We are a great imposition upon you, *monsieur*.'

'No, no, it is a pleasure, *madame*. Your servants do so much we scarcely notice you.'

'Your cook must notice the extra mouths to feed,' she said drily.

The doctor spread his hands.

'You pay for your food; your maid helps with the preparation and your coachman Wilson, he chops the logs: my cook is *très heureuse*. She remembers the old days when my wife was alive. We had a much larger household then, with many servants. She enjoys cooking for you all.'

'You are all most kind to us *monsieur*. Especially when it could be dangerous for you.'

'Do not distress yourself, *madame*. You have explained your dilemma and I have promised to help you. I have let it be known that your husband is a colleague of mine from England. That is why we have hidden the coach.' His eyes twinkled. 'No one would believe a humble country doctor would be acquainted with a marquis, eh?'

'Then it is only fitting that I should help with the household sewing,' she retorted, picking up another sheet.

* * *

It was another three days before there was any change in their situation. Rosamond was taking breakfast with Dr Sireuil when Davis came in to tell her that the marquis was awake and asking for her.

'Pray finish your coffee, *madame*,' murmured Dr Sireuil. 'He will not run away.'

Five minutes later she entered the bedchamber to find Lord Ullenwood propped up on a bank of pillows.

'Good morning, my lord.' She came forward, unable to conceal her pleasure at seeing him awake. 'Davis is to be congratulated. You are washed, brushed and shaved to perfection.'

'Baggage,' he said softly.

She sat down on the chair beside the bed.

'Are you in much pain, sir?'

'Only if I move my arm or shoulder.'

'I am very thankful that we met Dr Sireuil upon the road.'

'Yes, he has patched me up nicely. How long have we been here?'

'Almost a se'ennight, my lord.'

'And have you slept well, madam? Has your conscience been easy, leaving me to the mercies of my servants each night? Perhaps you were giving me my own again for not visiting you when you had that trifling chill.'

'No, sir. You were not lucid, and so full of laudanum we decided — '

'We decided?' He scowled at her. 'You are picking up revolutionary ideas, madam. The sooner I get you back to England the better!'

'Well, yes, so I think,' she replied cheerfully.

'The doctor has a friend near St Brieuc whom, he says, has — er — dubious sea-going contacts. It is a little further than St Malo, but I think we would be advised to accept the doctor's help. Also, he has suggested that we should leave our carriage here and he will arrange another less conspicuous vehicle for us.'

'By God, madam, you have been very busy while I have been asleep.'

'Making plans, my lord, yes, but we will do nothing without your approval.'

'I am very glad to hear it,' he growled. 'Is there nothing for me to do?'

'Yes, my lord: you must get well.' She rose. 'Now, here is Davis with your breakfast. With your permission, sir, I will go away.'

'And if I command you to stay?' His eyes challenged her. Rosamond found herself enjoying this new game.

'Then, of course, I would do so, my lord, although I fear we would incur your valet's displeasure, and I know he could make you *most* uncomfortable: is that not right, Davis?'

'My lord knows I exist only to do his bidding,' replied the valet smoothly.

The marquis gave a bark of laughter, cut short as the movement tore at his shoulder.

'The devil you do! Very well, madam, go away, but I want to you come and sit with me later, if only to stop you hatching more plans with my servants!'

* * *

Rosamond went to her room, humming, and found Meggie putting away her gowns.

'So the master is awake, ma'am. How is he?'

'Much better,' replied Rosamond, smiling at the memory of their verbal exchange. 'He is very well indeed.'

Rosamond soon discovered that Davis's prophecy was correct: the marquis was impatient to be up and about and it took the combined efforts of his doctor, his wife and his valet to keep him in his bed for even a few more days. Rosamond now had little time for household chores: she spent her days with the marquis, reading to him in French from the doctor's large supply of books, playing cards or, in the evenings, talking until the candles were guttering in their sockets.

* * *

As soon as Lord Ullenwood was well enough to leave his bed he began to talk of continuing their journey, but Rosamond would have none of it. Doctor Sireuil said it was too soon, the wounds were not healed enough to withstand the jolting of a coach over miles of uneven roads. Rosamond refused to leave. She watched the marquis pace up and down in his chamber, his injured arm resting in a sling.

'We should be moving. Every day we stay here the situation becomes more dangerous. And I have . . . messages to relay in England.'

'Since you will tell no one just what these messages are, it is important that we get you home alive,' she responded, very reasonably.

'Damnation, woman!' He strode up to her, towering over her.

Rosamond gazed up at him.

'So you will not obey me, madam, and make preparations to leave?'

'No, sir, I will not. Now, please return to your bed. The doctor will be here any moment.'

'I am damned if I will!'

'Then sit down, sir. You will do yourself no good to be moving so much.'

With a growl he lowered himself into the chair, wincing a little.

'Where is John?'

'Chopping wood.' She walked across the room to fetch a blanket. 'And pray do not think you will bully him into doing your bidding: I have given instructions that we are staying here until Dr Sireuil agrees that you are well enough to travel.'

'By God, then I shall turn them all off,' he threw at her. 'And you as well!'

'We are already agreed on that, my lord,' she said, tucking the blanket around his legs. 'I shall find them employment with me.'

He put out his good hand, taking her chin in his fingers and forcing her to look at him.

'I thought so,' he growled. 'You are laughing at me.'

She smiled at him, her hand coming up to cover his.

'No, sir, laughing *with* you: you cannot bamboozle me with your harsh words.'

His scowl fled.

'Am I so easy to understand, then?'

'Yes, now I have come to know you.'

His hand moved to her cheek, cradling it for a moment, but he withdrew it as the door opened. Rosamond straightened.

'Doctor Sireuil. Your patient is ready for you, you see.' She went to the door. Lord Ullenwood's voice followed her.

'You will return?'

'Later, my lord, when you have rested.'

The marquis swore softly as she left the room and before she closed the door she heard the doctor laugh.

'The ladies, they are tyrants are they not,

monsieur le marquis? Now, milor', let me look at your arm . . . '

* * *

Lord Ullenwood continued to recover quickly and a few days later Dr Sireuil agreed that he was fit enough to travel. Rosamond immediately gave instructions for the servants to begin packing up. Meggie sighed as she surveyed the open trunks.

'I vow, madam, soon you will have nothing left: first we had to leave behind half our belongings when we were reduced to one carriage, now you tell me we shall only be allowed to take one trunk with us back to England. How we are to decide what to take and what to leave heaven only knows!'

'We must make the best of it, Meggie. Pack only what is necessary and the rest I shall leave for the doctor to give to the poor. Come, Megs, cheer up, do: I cannot bear to see that Friday face!'

'I cannot see what there is to be so cheerful about,' grumbled her maid. 'The master wounded, the carriage lost and all of us returning home with little more than the clothes on our backs. Shameful, I calls it.'

Rosamond laughed. 'You are too gloomy, Meggie. Dr Sireuil is confident my lord will make a full recovery, and when we reach England, why, we shall have the pleasure of buying a carriage full of gowns. Think how entertaining that will be.'

Humming to herself, Rosamond went downstairs, where she found the marquis and their host in the doctor's surgery.

'Well, Rose,' said Lord Ullenwood as she entered, 'the good doctor has strapped my arm so securely to my chest there is no chance of it moving. He says it will be safer for the journey.'

'*Vraiment*, milor', you must do everything you can to keep your arm still. I have given your man instructions on what to do if he needs to change the dressing.'

'Yes, thank you. I will travel without my frock coat and my surcoat thrown over my injured shoulder — what do you think, Rose, will I pass as a wounded hero?'

Even though he was dressed only in his shirt, waistcoat and breeches Rosamond thought him every inch a handsome hero, but she was not about to tell him so. Instead she said, 'Meggie is finishing the packing now, my lord.'

'Good. John is already gone out to inspect the coach.'

'My apologies, milor', that it is not as luxurious as your English chariot,' said the doctor, 'However, it should carry you to St Brieuc, and attract little attention. With the moon and a clear sky, you will be able to travel through the night. I have given Wilson instructions on the best route to take and I have written a letter of introduction for you to give to Jean-Paul Diot when you reach St Brieuc.' He held the letter out to the marquis, who put up his hand.

'Perhaps, sir, you should give it to my wife. She has taken charge of this adventure.'

Rosamond blushed, laughed and stepped forward.

'Very well, my lord, if you insist on playing the invalid — '

The marquis reached out and took the letter even as her hand came up for it.

'In that case, I shall take it.' His eyes glinted at her. 'I am tired of playing the invalid, as you will discover very soon, my dear.'

Her blush deepened and, mumbling that she needed to speak to her maid, Rosamond hurried away.

* * *

At last everything was ready. The baggage was strapped to the carriage and Lady Ullenwood took an affectionate leave of the doctor, promising to write as soon as they were safely in England.

'I wish you God speed, milady.' The doctor kissed her hand. 'And to you, milor'. It might be best if you did not use your title when travelling through Brittany: in the present climate your rank might be held against you even more than your nationality.'

Lord Ullenwood bowed.

'You may be right, sir. We must use my family name. We shall be plain Mr and Mrs Malvern.'

The old man chuckled.

'Never plain, milor'. Never plain.'

With a final word of thanks Lord Ullenwood escorted Rosamond to the waiting coach. Davis climbed up on the box with John but Meggie was jammed in beside Rosamond and the marquis. Rosamond had insisted Lord Ullenwood should take a corner seat, with his injured shoulder resting against extra pillows to protect it as much as possible from the jolting of the carriage.

'It is the best I can do for you,' said Rosamond, following him into the carriage and adjusting the pillows behind him. 'With Meggie sitting with us it will be a squeeze, sir. I am sorry we cannot make you more comfortable.'

'It seems an ideal situation to me,' he

grinned, pulling her down beside him. Squashed in the far corner, Meggie huffed and shook her head.

'I don't know,' she muttered to herself, 'here we are, stuck in a foreign land, leaving behind everything we possess and neither of them is a whit concerned.'

The marquis reached for Rosamond's hand.

'We have lost a few bags, Meggie, that is all.'

'Humph!' said Meggie again. 'That is what my lady said.'

Lord Ullenwood grinned at his wife.

'When we get back we shall go to Bond Street and I will buy you a trousseau worthy of a bride.'

21

They travelled through the night with the full moon riding high above them in the clear sky, making the unfamiliar landscape even more alien by bathing everything in shades of blue and black. Rosamond tried to stay awake, but Elliot put his good arm about her and insisted she lean against him, her head resting on his shoulder. She dozed fitfully until the first streaks of dawn heralded a cold but sunny day.

When they stopped for breakfast at a busy roadside inn, the marquis suggested that he should take a turn on the box. His valet's impassive mask slipped for a moment.

'Good God no, my lord! If you will permit me to say so, with only one good arm you are not fit to drive, and should we run into trouble, I doubt you would manage the shot-gun.'

'He is right, sir,' said Rosamond, leading him into the inn. 'Davis is far more use than you would be on the box. I think John even condescends to let him handle the ribbons on the quieter stretches of the road.'

'A concession indeed,' replied the marquis.

'Davis will become so set up in his own importance there will be no bearing with him.'

Rosamond answered in kind, glad to encourage this lighter mood. She knew how much the infirmity irked her husband but Dr Sireuil had been at pains to stress that he must rest if his wounds were to heal properly. She was determined to follow his instructions.

* * *

Another full day's travel left them all exhausted, and Rosamond was thankful for the doctor's letter of introduction to the mayor of a small town on their route, which secured them accommodation for the night. Despite being shown every comfort, Rosamond saw that Lord Ullenwood was looking very grey and drawn when they set off again. She instructed John to keep a steady pace and avoid jolting the marquis any more than necessary. The coachman touched his hat.

'Aye, ma'am, I'll do that, but these dashed foreign roads is in such a bad state 'tis well nigh impossible to avoid all the ruts.'

'Well, I know you will do your best.'

She watched the marquis closely as the day

wore on, but although he appeared pale, he did not seem to grow any worse. She was thankful when they reached St Brieuc and found rooms at a busy inn, where Lord Ullenwood was well enough to conduct negotiations. Rosamond watched anxiously, but their host was only interested in knowing they had the means to pay their way. He had seen too many fashionable families in reduced circumstances to be curious.

'The landlord is preparing separate rooms for us, my dear,' said the marquis, escorting her into the inn and to an empty table. 'He appeared to think we would expect it, and I did not disillusion him.'

A waitress dressed *en paysanne* brought them wine, and by the time she had withdrawn, Rosamond had thought better of uttering the protest that rose to her lips. The closeness that they had developed during their stay with Dr Sireuil had faded once they were on the road. The marquis had become morose and taciturn. She had attributed it to the exhausting journey and frustration at his continued weakness, but she was pained by his refusal to confide in her and his cool acceptance of a separate room only confirmed her belief that he wanted to put an end to their marriage.

Since Rosamond had been the one to

suggest an annulment, it seemed churlish that she should resent his efforts to protect her, but she *did* resent it and snapping at Meggie only increased her discontent.

* * *

A dull, wet morning did not revive her spirits, but a message that the marquis would call to escort her downstairs raised a smile. She allowed Meggie to dress her hair, buttoned the jacket of her tightly fitting travelling dress and was ready for him when the knock fell upon the door. As Meggie opened it, she gasped. The marquis bowed.

'Good morning, madam. I have done away with the sling, as you can see.' Lord Ullenwood stepped into the room. He was wearing his blue driving jacket, buckskins and top boots and at first glance appeared to have no injury. As he walked into the room, however, she noticed that he did not move his left arm.

'How did you manage to pull your coat over your bandages?' she asked him suspiciously.

'Davis replaced them all this morning: the arm is much better and did not require so much binding. And, thankfully, I have never wanted my coats so tight that I cannot dress without the aid of my valet, so the sleeve fitted quite well. So, my lady, may I escort you downstairs?'

'You know I would not have countenanced your leaving off your sling, had I known,' she remarked as they took their seats at the table.

The marquis merely smiled and waited until they had been served with coffee and rolls before replying.

'I had the devil of a task to persuade Davis to help me. I knew if you had been present he would have proved even more difficult.'

'I see.' She played with her coffee cup. 'Is that why you were so pleased to have separate chambers?'

'In part.' He reached out and caught her hand. 'Rose, I promised you we would not discuss our marriage until we reached England, but I must say something. I confess I have been tempted to take you to my bed a dozen times, and if I had not been injured I may well have done so by now.'

'But we were together some weeks before you were shot,' she pointed out, trying not to sound angry.

He sat back.

'Ah yes. You put me under an obligation, Rose.'

'I did?' she eyed him doubtfully.

'Yes. When I offered for you I thought it a

very practical arrangement. We would be wed, you would provide me with an heir and we would go about our own lives. But soon after we agreed upon the marriage you told me that since your grandfather's death I was your only friend. From that moment it became important to me to make you happy. I was determined not to force myself upon you, or to hurt you.' His lip curled. 'So it has turned out for the best: you are still a maid and I must make sure you remain so. For me to touch you even once would be fatal to your chances of an annulment and I would not put you through the ignominy of a divorce.'

'Oh,' she said, in a small voice.

He squeezed her fingers before releasing them.

'These are extraordinary circumstances, Rose. I would not have you do anything you might regret once we are back in Society.'

'Oh,' she said again.

She sipped her coffee, trying to make sense of the whirl of emotions his words had conjured within her. His kindness touched her, and if he was to be believed, then his forbearance was entirely for her sake. When they reached England she could make her choice whether or not to continue with the marriage. But it would not do: she was no nearer to knowing what *he* wanted.

She looked up to find he was watching her. Her heart tightened at the sight of him, the black hair, sleek as a raven's wing, his handsome face smiling at her now with so much warmth that she wondered how she had ever thought him cold and arrogant. He deserved so much more that she could give him: he deserved to make a brilliant match, one that would please his aunts and bring honour and fortune to his family.

'What is it, Rose?'

She swallowed and shook her head. It was a struggle to speak, but she managed three words.

'Nothing of importance.'

'Very well, let us discuss our next move. After we have broken our fast I think we should seek out this acquaintance of Sireuil's, Monsieur Diot. Will you come with me?'

'Of course.'

22

Their enquiries led them to an apothecary's shop where they presented the doctor's letter to Monsieur Diot, the owner, and were quickly shown into the back room, where they were pressed to take a glass of wine with the family and asked many questions about Dr Sireuil and his sister. Rosamond did her best to answer before the apothecary sent his family away and asked Lord Ullenwood to explain their situation. He listened intently, nodding occasionally. When the marquis had finished describing their flight from Paris, Monsieur Diot nodded.

'Well, Monsieur Malvern, I see why my old friend has sent you to me. I will make all the arrangements, *monsieur*, but it will take some days. You must go back to the inn and remain there. Tell them you are come to visit the cathedral. It was named after a Welsh saint, I believe.'

He showed them to the door.

'I will send word as soon as I can.'

* * *

There followed a tense few days waiting for news. None of them could be easy, but Rosamond drew some comfort from knowing that the marquis's wounds were healing rapidly, now that they had stopped travelling. At last word came, and on a blustery spring morning they set off from St Brieuc, across the river and heading north-west towards the coast. Monsieur Diot was waiting for them at the crossroads just outside the town. He was mounted on a long-tailed hack and led the way down winding lanes to a small inlet that boasted a few boats, half-a-dozen houses and a small, run-down inn. A stocky, bearded man came out of the inn and a short conversation took place with Monsieur Diot. It was carried out at speed and in a dialect Rosamond could not understand, but when the apothecary brought the man to the carriage and introduced him, she was relieved that his French, although heavily accented, was understandable.

'Henri will look after you now.' Monsieur Diot gathered up his reins. '*Adieu, m'sieur, madame*. It may be necessary for you to remain at the inn for a few nights, to wait for a crossing, but you will be perfectly safe here.' He touched his hat and with a final nod he rode away, leaving them to follow Henri to the inn.

⋆ ⋆ ⋆

'Oh my lordy, never say we are to sail in one of those little tubs!' cried Meggie, looking in horror at the small fishing boats moored at the edge of the water.

'I would sail in a nutshell if it would get me to England,' declared Rosamond. They were passing a group of fishwives, cleaning the day's catch. Rosamond heard them cackling and understood enough of their speech to hear them remark that the full-bodied serving maid would make good ballast if the crossing was a rough one. Rosamond thought it best not to translate this for Meggie.

⋆ ⋆ ⋆

The inn boasted only two rooms, and the marquis insisted that Meggie and Rosamund share one of the rooms while he took the other with John and Davis. He caught sight of Meggie's scandalized face and laughed.

'Your maid thinks me quite sunk beyond reproach to be sharing a room with Davis and John,' he said. 'What would you have me do, order my servants to sleep outside?'

'Of course not. Pray do not tease Meggie,' returned Rosamond, trying not to smile. 'You accused me of showing revolutionary tendencies: it seems that you too share them.'

He flicked her cheek with a careless finger. 'I am once more amazed how alike we are.'

* * *

The food at the inn was simple fare, but well cooked and presented by Henri's wife, who confided to Rosamond that she had at one time been a kitchen maid at one of the grand houses.

'How long will we have to wait for a crossing, do you think?' Lord Ullenwood asked her when they sat down to dinner for the second night. They were alone at the inn, but still the woman looked about her before answering.

'We are in the hands of the gods, *m'sieur*. The ship, he must wait for the tide and the wind, but he will come, you will see.'

* * *

The following night they were woken from their beds by the news that an English lugger was in the harbour.

'*Vite, vite*,' hissed the landlady, coming into Rosamond's chamber and lighting the lamp. 'He is unloading now, and will take you back with him.'

The thought of being in England once more acted as a spur to Rosamond and Meggie, who quickly made their way down to the taproom where the others were waiting. Their trunk was corded up and carried down to the water. A sliver of moon was riding high in the sky, and Rosamond was grateful they did not have to depend upon the feeble light of their guide's lantern to show them the way. As she walked with the marquis towards the lugger she was surprised to see so many figures moving in the darkness. On one side sailors and villagers were working to offload barrels and packages that were then slung across the backs of a string of pack-ponies while on the other more barrels were being loaded onto the deck. Henri came up to them, a broad-shouldered giant following him.

'This is Branscombe, captain of the lugger,' he said, jerking his head in the direction of the giant, who stepped forward and said in a rich, West-Country drawl, 'We's full to the rigging tonight, sir. But you and your party's welcome to come aboard, as long as 'ee don't mind passing the journey on deck. There's a fair wind blowin' so I reckons we should be in Devon in about eight hours.'

Meggie groaned quietly and Rosamond gripped her hand, willing her to be brave. She kept silent as a bargain was struck, their trunk was taken on board and very soon they were following the captain along the narrow boards that acted as a quay and were being helped aboard ship.

'Lawks, miss, is it safe?' whispered Meggie. 'It seems so small to be going out to sea.'

One of the sailors overheard and turned to give them a toothless grin.

'Lordy,' he chuckled. 'Don't 'ee be worryin' about the *Falcon*, missy. She's a fifteen-ton lugger, and with a thousand square foot o' canvas spread, she'll have 'ee back 'ome in no time.'

⋆ ⋆ ⋆

Captain Branscombe showed them to an area of the deck where they were assured they would be in no one's way.

'Everywhere else it's barrels or sails and riggin' that me lads need to work with, and there'll be no by-your-leave if you gets in the way.'

John sat down on a nearby barrel and took out his pipe.

'Methinks we'd be best to stay put then.'

The others made themselves comfortable on the deck, wrapped in their thick travelling cloaks. Around them the crew was busy loading the remaining cargo and making preparations to put to sea again.

'Goodness!' Rosamond looked around, wide-eyed. 'Can all this be contraband?'

The marquis came to sit beside her.

'Undoubtedly. I suspect our fine captain is a free-trader.'

'How exciting.'

He laughed.

'You should be shocked, madam.'

'It is impossible for me to condemn someone who is helping us. Besides, one is always reading the newspaper reports that most of the tea and brandy we drink in England has never paid duty.' She watched, fascinated, as the signals were given to put to sea. She looked back, watching the tiny pinpoints of light from the harbour lanterns growing smaller. As they left the shelter of the inlet the wind grew stronger and the marquis suggested they should sit down on the deck so that the barrels would provide some shelter.

Remembering their outward journey, Rosamond was concerned that Meggie might succumb to sea sickness again, but her maid was quick to reassure her.

'Why, miss, I'm right as my glove sitting here on the deck! It is very different being up here in the air, you see, from being in a closed cabin.'

Davis too seemed to be surviving the voyage, sitting next to John Wilson and showing no signs of his previous sickness.

The little vessel settled into a steady motion and when there was light enough to see, the only view in any direction was the grey water and a clear sky. The captain came over to them, rolling with the ship as he walked.

'Is all well with you and yours, Mr Malvern, sir?' He accepted a pinch of snuff from the marquis and sat down beside him, ready to repay this sign of comradeship with conversation.

Rosamond was fascinated and by gentle questioning she persuaded the man to tell her something of his trade. The marquis, amused, sat back and became an observer.

'Well, we've a mixed cargo on board tonight, ma'am. Half-ankers of Cousin Jack — that's barrels of brandy to you, ma'am, and silks and spices safe below-deck.'

'And what would happen if you were caught?' asked Rosamond.

The captain grinned.

'Why, bless you, ma'am, they give us plenty o' warning. There's no cutter could creep up on a man out here. No, if the Revenue cutter hoves into view and gives chase, well then we just sow the crop — rope the half-ankers together, weight ’em with stones and drop ’em overboard.’

‘But how would you know where you had dropped them?’ asked Meggie, looking at the endless expanse of grey water.

‘There’s charts, miss, that we can mark and then we come back later to pick up our cargo, but we cannot be leaving it too long, else the sea water will get into the barrels and spoil the brandy.’

‘And when you land,’ said Rosamond, intrigued, ‘surely there is more chance there of you being surprised?’

‘Aye, madam, but we have lookouts who give us the nod if there’s trouble. For instance, when we are standing off the bay you look to the cliff top, and if you see a man on a grey horse riding south along the cliff, then you know we’ll be safe to land.’

‘Should you be telling us all this, Captain?’ murmured the marquis. ‘Can we be trusted, do you think?’

The giant threw back his head and gave a hearty bellow of laughter.

‘I’ve only told ’ee what the Revenue men already knows, sir. And as for the lookout, that changes every trip, so much good that information will do ’ee.’

With a nod the captain went off, still chuckling.

* * *

Snuggled down behind the barrels and sheltered from the wind, Rosamond closed her eyes, enjoying the warm sun on her face. Occasionally, the spray would touch her skin, but it did not disturb her and with her companions she dozed for the remainder of the crossing until a quiet word from the marquis made her sit up. They were within sight of land, the rugged cliffs and green hills of the Devon coast growing ever closer.

The marquis pointed.

'That is our destination, I think,' he said. 'That small cleft in the hills. And there, if I am not mistaken, is the lookout.'

She followed his outstretched finger, looking up at the cliff top. A tiny figure, a rider on a grey horse, could be seen riding along the ridge.

'He is heading south. That means it is clear.' She turned to the marquis. 'We are home, Elliot.'

He put his arm around her and pulled her to him. Before she knew it he was kissing her. It was rough and salty, the full day's growth of stubble on his chin grazed her face but she wanted it to go on forever. Her hand came up, fingers threading through his dark hair. At last he let her go, but only so that he could look down into her face.

'That is the first time you have used my name,' he murmured.

'Really? I did not notice.'

He hugged her. 'I hope you will continue to use it, Rose. I like the sound of it on your lips.'

The cliffs were towering over them now, the sun almost directly overhead.

'I thought we should be landing here on a moonless night,' confessed Rosamond.

Davis allowed himself a rare smile.

'The captain says these remote beaches are quite safe, even in daylight.'

They were heading towards the narrow strip of beach at the mouth of the inlet, where a string of pack-horses was already waiting. The captain sailed the shallow-keeled lugger directly on to the beach, leaving only a few feet of water to be negotiated. The men had removed their boots and jumped down to wade ashore while Meggie was subjected to the indignity of being thrown over the captain's shoulder to save wetting her thick skirts. Rosamond submitted herself to the same treatment and was soon standing on the beach beside the marquis, a little red-faced, but perfectly composed. The captain wished them good fortune for the remainder of their journey. Lord Ullenwood handed him a purse which he pocketed with a word of thanks and a wink, adding, 'I'll have one of the village lads escort you to the vicarage. The parson will be able to take you in until you can arrange for a carriage to carry you back to London.'

'I might need to find a banker first,' the marquis replied. 'My ready funds are nigh exhausted.'

'Well, once the dibs are in tune we should be able to find ourselves a decent carriage and horses now, my lord,' remarked John, tapping out his pipe and refilling it.

The captain cocked an enquiring eyebrow. 'My lord?'

'Marquis of Ullenwood, at your service, Captain.' Elliot bowed. 'It was thought advisable not to use the title in France.'

'No, very true,' muttered the captain, staring at him for a moment before grinning broadly. 'Well, dang me! So I've had a real live marquis on board. Well I never!'

He walked away, chuckling, and Lord Ullenwood took Rosamond's arm and began to follow a ragged urchin to the vicarage, leaving Meggie to follow behind with Davis and John, who were waiting for their trunk to be secured on a spare pack-horse.

* * *

They had not quite left the beach when the marquis looked behind him to see that the others were out of earshot.

'Well, Rose, I am too impatient to wait any longer. It is time to make some decisions,' he said. 'You have become such a managing female these past weeks that it should not be hard for you.'

'What is there to decide, my lord?'

'In Paris, madam, you were determined our marriage was a mistake and must be annulled. I need to know if you want me to take you to London and summon our lawyers, or do we go directly to Leverhill?'

She swallowed.

'What — what would you like to do, Elliot?'

He stopped and turned towards her, catching her hands. His thumbs circled the bare patch of skin between glove and sleeve, sending little shockwaves up her arms, and making it even more difficult for her to stand still.

'Wiltshire is, of course, closer.'

At his words she gave an exasperated sigh and his grip tightened. 'Forgive me.' He fixed his eyes at some point above her head and said carefully, 'I was ever a solitary man, Rose. I have never been in the habit of explaining myself and do not find it easy to share my thoughts with anyone. It is especially difficult now, when it concerns something so close to my heart. You have never seen Leverhill. I think you would like it. We will be too late to see the spring flowers, but the bluebells in the home wood look wonderful. My father had Leverhill built for his bride and I have always thought of it as home.' He looked down at her. 'We have made a poor beginning, Rose. I would like us to start again: this time it will be a real marriage, for both of us.'

'But you said we should go our own way, my lord,' she reminded him. 'It was to be a marriage of convenience, a logical choice: you could have your mistresses and I — '

She broke off as the grip on her hands became painful.

'Logic be damned!' he retorted savagely. 'I was foolish ever to think of it. If we are to continue, madam, there will be no one else, on either side. I will make you this promise, Rose: in future there will be no mistress in my life except you.' He stopped. She observed the muscle in his cheek working and she wanted to reach up to smooth away his worried look, to tell him she understood, but she needed him to tell her what was in his heart. He continued, 'I should like to take you home with me now, to have and to hold, from this day forward. What do you say, Rose?'

She looked down at their clasped hands.

'You said that only a fool would seek perfection, sir, but would I be too much of a fool to expect you to — to love me?'

'To — Well, of course I do!'

'You have never told me so.'

He put his fingers under her chin and tilted her face up towards him. 'My darling Rose, I love you more than life itself. I love you, if you must know, to the point of madness!'

She blinked, but this time the tears would not be held back. They spilled over her cheeks, even while her face was wreathed in smiles.

'Oh Elliot, my love, I have wanted you to say that for so long!'

He kissed her.

'Well, then, madam, which is it to be? Make your choice.'

With a happy sigh she leaned against him.

'Take me home, Elliot.'

23

Lord and Lady Ullenwood returned to London in September in time for the wedding of Mrs Tomlinson to Sir James Ashby. They arrived at Ullenwood House to find Arabella waiting for them. As they entered the salon she ran forward, chattering non-stop.

'Cousin Elliot, how well you look! And Rose, my love, let me look at you. I declare you are positively blooming! We have been longing to see you, for although your letters explaining how you escaped from France were fascinating, my dear, there is so much I want to ask you, and you do not need to worry at all that I did not get my dashy dress, for I have found the most wonderful French seamstress here in Town. My love, would you credit it? Oh, and Mama was obliged to go out, but she says I am to make sure I thank you for allowing us to live at Ullenwood House until the wedding. She is so happy to be hostess here, but all that will have to change now you are come, of course . . . '

The marquis walked over to Sir James, who was leaning heavily on a cane.

'Good God, Ashby, do you really want to marry such a gabster?'

'Isn't she a darling?' Sir James grinned. 'She is excited, that is all. Were you surprised when you heard we were betrothed? I hope you do not object?'

Lord Ullenwood put out his hand.

'Would it make a difference if I did object? My wife guessed which way the wind was blowing, so I was prepared. Congratulations, my friend. And I am glad to see you up and about again.'

Sir James gripped his hand.

'Thank you, Elliot. But tell me, how are you, fully recovered now I trust?'

'Aye, never better. Spending the summer at Leverhill has been perfect for us both.'

'From what I learned of your time in France I think you deserved it. The message you sent to me, that Napoleon had decided to sell Louisiana and concentrate on building up his western ports, finally convinced the government to act. Very late, of course, but it could have been much worse.'

'So we are at war again, and in imminent expectation of invasion.'

'Aye, but better that than to be shilly-shallying while Bonaparte has it all his own way. We have pre-empted him, Elliot. Personally, I do not believe Boney will try to invade us now. We spiked his guns. Let me pour you some of this excellent cognac, my friend.'

'Thank you,' Lord Ullenwood's lips twitched. 'It is mine own, after all. And after the events of the spring I have a special affection for the spirit. So, how are the arrangements proceeding for your wedding?'

'Very well, my friend. Bella and her mother discuss everything with my own dear mama: there is nothing for me to do but to turn up on the day.'

'And Lady Ashby's ball, to celebrate your forthcoming nuptials?'

'All arranged for Friday, as planned.'

The marquis studied his glass.

'And the guest list — you have added my suggestions?'

Sir James grinned.

'Yes. Mama was dead set against it, of course, but you are after all the hero of the hour, and your wishes must be granted.'

'Excellent. Then we can look forward to an eventful evening.'

* * *

Rosamond was at her dressing-table when the marquis came in. She looked up, meeting his eyes in the mirror. Her heart swelled with pride at the sight of him in his black evening coat, white waistcoat and the tight knee breeches that showed his muscled thighs to advantage.

'Is it time to leave already, my lord? I am sorry, I thought — '

'No, calm yourself, my love. You have plenty of time. I came to see how you go on.' He put his hands on her shoulders, smiling at her in the mirror. 'What is it, my love: do you not wish to go to Lady Ashby's ball?'

She sighed.

'Bella is my dearest friend, and Sir James has been your close companion since you were boys. You know we must attend, it is in their honour.'

'And I want the opportunity to show off my new bride. You have not yet been to a Society ball, Rose. You might enjoy it.'

She thought back to her last public appearance in Paris, and her cheeks reddened at the memory. She dropped her head to one side, resting her cheek on his hand.

'I am sure I shall, if you are there beside me.'

He kissed her neck.

'Good girl. Now, I have brought you this.'

She took the slim leather case and opened it carefully, gasping as the light glittered on the diamonds nestling on their satin bed.

'Oh, Elliot, they are beautiful.'

He lifted out the necklace and fastened it around her neck.

'Wear this for me tonight, with the matching ear-drops . . . there, now stand up and let me look at you.'

She rose and stood before him, shaking out the skirts of her white and silver gown.

'Will I do for you, Elliot? I do not wish to let you down.'

He picked up her spangled shawl and draped it gently over her shoulders.

'You look magnificent, my dear. And you must not be anxious. I shall be at your side throughout the evening, I promise you.'

* * *

Ashby House was on the western fringe of the capital, a pristine new building with soaring white columns at its impressive entrance. When the Ullenwood town coach arrived at the sweeping drive it was already crowded and it took several minutes for them to reach the shallow steps where liveried footmen jumped forward to open the door and tenderly help them to alight. Lady Ashby, Sir James and Arabella were waiting at the top of the grand staircase and, as Rosamond approached, Lady Ashby held out her be-ringed hands to her.

'So you are Elliot's new bride. At last we meet. How do you do, my dear? Such adventures as you have had! James has told me all about it, not that he needed to do so, because it is all over Town, you know. You and Elliot will be much fêted tonight, I think. But I suppose I must not keep you with me. Off you go, now and talk to Arabella.'

As Rosamond moved away she turned to Lord Ullenwood.

'Well, well, Elliot. No wonder you are looking so pleased with yourself — your bride is adorable.'

'Thank you, ma'am.'

'And do your aunts approve?'

'They do, my lady. I took Lady Ullenwood to visit each of 'em during the summer.'

She tapped his arm.

'Much you would care if they disapproved of your choice!'

'True, but my wife would care, so I am glad they like her.'

'Hmm, you seem very fond of your new bride, which makes it all the more puzzling why you should ask me to add that woman to my guest list. But there, all the world and his wife will be here tonight, so I doubt we shall even notice her.'

He smiled.

'Oh I think we will, ma'am.'

* * *

Everywhere she went Rosamond found people wanting to be presented to her and to talk about their escape from France. Elliot was true to his word and stayed with her and Rosamond began to relax and enjoy herself. She refused to dance, excusing herself on the grounds that she was still in mourning, but she was happy to stand beside her husband, watching James and Arabella.

'You would not know his leg had been so badly broken last winter,' she marvelled, watching him perform a lively gavotte with his fiancée.

The music stopped and she joined in the polite applause.

'I was so pleased when Arabella wrote to tell me they were betrothed,' she said. 'I am sure — '

She broke off, staring at the door. The blood was pounding in her ears and if it had not been for Elliot's supporting arm she thought her legs might have collapsed beneath her. A hush had fallen over the room, and all eyes were fixed upon the figure standing in the doorway.

* * *

Mrs Lythmore paused, pleased with the effect of her late arrival. She was magnificently attired in a gown of gold lustring with matching turban and nodding gold plumes. It had cost a pretty penny, but she had thought it worthwhile to invest in a new gown for Lady Ashby's ball. Invitations had not been so plentiful recently, but she had come back to Town after spending the summer with Harry Granthorpe at his Sussex estate to find Lady Ashby's gilt-edged card waiting for her. Never before had the doors of Ashby House been opened to her, but Sir James had always been thick with the Marquis of Ullenwood: this could only mean one thing; Elliot had tired of his little ingénue and wanted her back.

Now, surveying the hushed ballroom, the surprised faces, she felt a moment of triumph. It was fashionable of course to make a late entrance, and she had always been at the height of fashion. She ignored the cold stares of Sir James and his future bride and made her way toward the marquis. She hardly noticed the pale little figure at his side. Why should she? After all, she was a nonentity.

Barbara Lythmore curtsied to her hostess, who offered her the slightest of nods, then she turned to the marquis.

'Good evening, my lord.'

'I was wondering if you would have the temerity to come.' Lord Ullenwood's tone was cold and he deliberately turned away from her to say to his wife, 'Come, my love. I believe it is cooler on the terrace. Let me fetch your wrap for you.'

The snub was unmistakable. Mrs Lythmore's eyes blazed with fury but she kept her smile and turned towards the other guests. Every way she moved they turned their backs on her, refusing even to acknowledge her presence. Only Sir James remained facing her, his fiancée at his side, looking disdainful.

'You should know, madam,' said Sir James, 'that your exploits in France have become legendary while you have been out of Town. Oh, don't blame Ullenwood,' he continued as she cast a fulminating glance towards the marquis. 'It was the ambassador who informed us of your — ah — privileged standing with Bonaparte and his ministers. That was shocking enough, madam, but to lay information against your own people — that is unforgivable.'

'Aye,' muttered someone nearby. 'Shameful.'

'But I did nothing — it is a lie!' she cried desperately.

A figure came forward from the crowd and she found herself facing Lord Whitworth.

'An ambassador must of necessity have many contacts,' he said slowly. 'Did you think I should not discover who had accused a loyal Englishman and his wife?'

The murmurs were growing. Mutterings of 'shame' and 'traitor' became louder. Mrs Lythmore looked around her, searching the crowd for a friendly face. There was none: even Harry Granthorpe turned his shoulder. With a shriek of annoyance she picked up her skirts and fled from the room.

Silence followed her departure, then a gradual return of conversation. Lady Ashby instructed the musicians to strike up again and moments later the couples were dancing. James and Arabella came out to join Rosamond and her husband on the terrace.

'Did you see the whole?' demanded Arabella.

'Yes.' Rosamond sighed. 'I found it quite chilling.'

Arabella shook her head. 'And now, everything is as it was: almost as if it never happened.'

Rosamond looked up at the marquis.

'Did you plan this, my lord? If so, it was quite reprehensible of you.'

'Do you mean to be severe, Rose? No, I did not exactly plan this. Let us say rather that I suggested she should be invited. Only a woman of immense conceit would have accepted.'

'Almost, I am sorry for her,' murmured Rosamond, as Sir James and Arabella wandered off into the darkened gardens.

'Do not be. Bad enough that she should seek to harm me, but her treatment of you demanded some retribution,' said Lord Ullenwood. 'This, I think, was just. She may find it hard to persuade a man to become her protector now.'

'Oh, I would not be too sure,' murmured Rosamond. 'The best of men can be such fools over a pretty face. History bears this out: Helen of Troy, Delilah, Lady MacBeth.'

He pulled her into his arms.

'Does history show us that men can become besotted with their own wives?'

Her eyes twinkled but she replied very gravely, 'Decidedly not, my lord.'

He hugged her closer.

'Well then, baggage,' he said, his eyes glinting menacingly, 'I think I shall have to be the exception that proves the rule!'

1	31	61	91	121	151	181	211	241	271	301	331
2	32	62	92	122	152	182	212	242	272	302	332
3	33	63	93	123	153	183	213	243	273	303	333
4	34	64	94	124	154	184	214	244	274	304	334
5	35	65	95	125	155	185	215	245	275	305	335
6	36	66	96	126	156	186	216	246	276	306	336
7	37	67	97	127	157	187	217	247	277	307	337
8	38	68	98	128	158	188	218	248	278	308	338
9	39	69	99	129	159	189	219	249	279	309	339
10	40	70	100	130	160	190	220	250	280	310	340
11	41	71	101	131	161	191	221	251	281	311	341
12	42	72	102	132	162	192	222	252	282	312	342
13	43	73	103	133	163	193	223	253	283	313	343
14	44	74	104	134	164	194	224	254	284	314	344
15	45	75	105	135	165	195	225	255	285	315	345
16	46	76	106	136	166	196	226	256	286	316	346
17	47	77	107	137	167	197	227	257	287	317	347
18	48	78	108	138	168	198	228	258	288	318	348
19	49	79	109	139	169	199	229	259	289	319	349
20	50	80	110	140	170	200	230	260	290	320	350
21	51	81	111	141	171	201	231	261	291	321	351
22	52	82	112	142	172	202	232	262	292	322	352
23	53	83	113	143	173	203	233	263	293	323	353
24	54	84	114	144	174	204	234	264	294	324	354
25	55	85	115	145	175	205	235	265	295	325	355
26	56	86	116	146	176	206	236	266	296	326	356
27	57	87	117	147	177	207	237	267	297	327	357
28	58	88	118	148	178	208	238	268	298	328	358
29	59	89	119	149	179	209	239	269	299	329	359
30	60	90	120	150	180	210	240	270	300	330	360